belle MEDIA

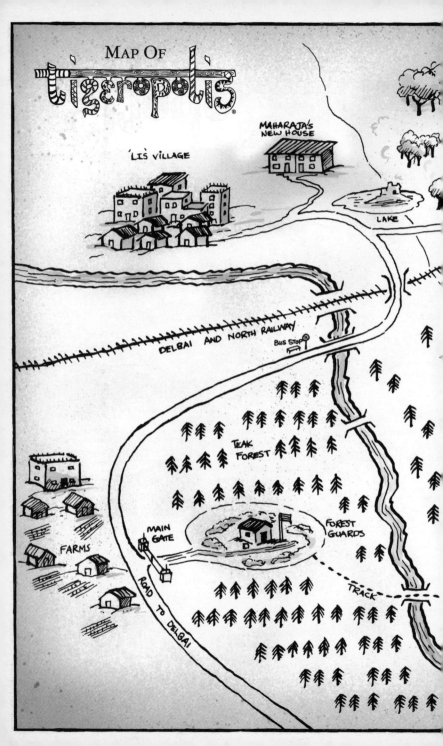

Welcome to the World of Tigeropolis

The Audiobooks

The Game

The Comic Strip

www.tigeropolis.co.uk

This book is dedicated to all the forest guards,
rangers, policemen, conservation experts, scientists,
and volunteers who have dedicated their lives to
protecting India's rich and diverse wildlife,
and in particular its magnificent *tigers*.

BOOK 2
THE GRAND OPENING

BY R.D. DIKSTRA

Copyright 2016 – R. D. Dikstra

First published in Great Britain in 2016 by Belle Media Ltd

The right of R. D. Dikstra to be identified as author of the work has been
asserted by him in accordance with the Copyright, Design and Patents Act 1988.

Tigeropolis is a Registered Trade Mark

Tigeropolis: a Belle Media Book

ISBN Number 978-0-9927462-2-3

Illustrations by Matt Rowe
Designed by Andrew Cook, essense design
Tigeropolis title design by Grace Anderson
Printed and bound in the UK by Clays Ltd, St Ives plc

Published by Belle Media Ltd, London
36 Ferry Quays, 5 Ferry Lane, London, TW8 0AT

Tel +44 (0)20 8568 3556
www.bellemedia.co.uk

Tigeropolis — Previously...

Tigeropolis is a mythical wildlife park at the foothills of the Himalayas. In Book 1, *Beyond the Deep Forest*, the tigers discovered that their idyllic life was under threat.

They enjoyed a tranquil life out of sight, but there was a price to pay: with no reported sightings for several years, the park authorities assumed the tigers had moved away. To them it was simple: no tigers meant no tourists and that, in turn, meant no income. Tigeropolis would have to close; the trees bulldozed, and in its place a new motorway built.

Bittu, Matti, Tala and Uncle Raj set out to save the park. They realised they needed to reappear, to create a vibrant tiger-watching tourist industry. There was just one small snag... it had been so long since any of them had appeared in public, that they had quite forgotten what to do. They needed to rediscover old skills quickly: how to roar and how to hunt.

With a little help from some unexpected quarters, they quickly relearnt the 'tricks of the trade' and saved the park.

We join them again as the forest rangers start planning for '*The Grand Opening*'...

Chapter 1 – The Invitation

'A VIP lunch for thirty?' exclaimed Forest Officer Mistry, clutching the Forest Department letter he had received from Delbai. 'Where on Earth are we going to hold that?' he complained.

'Oh dear,' said Akash, in sympathy with his colleague, 'Typical Delbai, sitting in their air-conditioned offices with absolutely no idea what we have to cope with. The chowki hut is only just big enough for the two of us.'

'Hmmm, the two of us and your weekly supplies of chocolate cake,' added the forest officer, looking around at all the dirty plates.

'Ha-ha, very funny…' said Akash, instinctively licking his lips at the very mention of chocolate cake.

Mr Mistry looked at Akash. 'The opening is just under two weeks away and the Minister is definitely coming. What are we going to do?' he said, desperate for some inspiration.

They sat in silence for a few moments, both thinking hard, then Akash smiled. 'Why don't we hold it at the old forest rest-house? It's got a large veranda and great views towards the river.'

'A bit tumbledown isn't it?' said Mr Mistry, 'But not altogether a bad idea.' He was not entirely convinced but, then again, he was getting rather desperate, and the invitations would have to be sent out in the next few days.

The forest rest-house was about two kilometres from the chowki hut and hadn't been used in years. It had been built in Victorian times, and was one of hundreds used by District Officers as they rode around the country on their monthly inspection tours. They were basic: simple whitewashed mud brick, thatched roof huts, with a small bedroom on each side of a central communal area, opening out onto a large veranda. All rather functional.

To the casual observer, they looked very much like an old English country railway station; something you might find in a 1930s murder mystery, rather than in a tiger park in Northern India. All that was missing was a passing steam train, and a little old stationmaster watering his begonias, while all sorts of dastardly deeds took place around him.

'Might work, I suppose,' said Mr Mistry, coming round to the idea for the want of anything better. 'But it will need some urgent tidying up. Last time I was there it was inhabited by a herd of goats. I'll get on to Mr Singh and see if he can do the food.'

Ten minutes later, he put down the receiver and turned to Akash. 'Well, hopefully that's sorted. A sit down lunch for thirty, and all for only 750 rupees a head. Oh, and he said he will see to the goats… in fact he seemed quite keen on sorting them out. He's even happy to do us a nice meat kebab for the price,' and with that, he swung his feet up onto the desk and settled down for a short nap, his day's work done.

'So…' Bittu thought to himself, getting down from what had now become his regular spot outside the chowki hut window. 'Now we know: First of October. Not long for us to get ready.' He set off immediately to tell the others what was planned.

'First of October?' said Raj, 'They're taking a bit of a chance with the weather: the end of the monsoon. Tricky one to forecast… what if the rains are still beating down? I can't see the Minister being pleased with that.

'And a Saturday too! Not sure they'll get many officials turning up on a weekend…' Raj continued, marking it down on the calendar.

'Oh, I don't know,' replied Tala. 'I think they might. It's so lovely here. I'm sure people will find plenty of excuses to come… and after all they're being invited out to the country for a big party, with a slap-up tea and all expenses paid.'

'Perhaps you're right.' said Raj, 'But surely they can't be serious about holding it at the forest rest-house! It's a ruin! Not been used since the last war. No running water. Last I saw, the goats were using it as a toilet! No, this has to be a big event with the Minister and all sorts of dignitaries coming… We need to be seen as India's number one tiger park. The rest-house? No… we'd be a laughing stock! We need something much better.'

He continued on his theme, getting more and more frustrated and upset at the thought of what was planned. 'It's supposed to be about promoting us: the newly discovered Tigeropolis tigers; not a reality TV show where they turn an old wreck into a luxury holiday hideaway by adding new curtains and a plastic chandelier!

'No, no, no… this just won't do… not at all. We need to take immediate action. We need somewhere impressive that grabs the attention.'

'What about the lake?' ventured Bittu.

'Ah yes, the lake… that's a possibility. It's certainly a nice view. But perhaps a bit too much like every other tiger park, in every other tourist brochure,' said Raj. 'We need somewhere that stands out… somewhere that instantly says… Tigeropolis,' moving his paw slowly through the air as if writing the name up in lights.

'The temple grounds?' Tala suggested a little hesitantly.

'Or… better still…' shouted Matti, leaping out excitedly from behind the settee, where she had been playing with her maharaja and princess doll set, 'What about… the Maharaja's old palace?'

'That's a perfect idea, Matti!' exclaimed Tala. 'The old palace would make an ideal background: the pink stone in the late afternoon light, the blue sky, fairy lights glistening on top of the minarets… It's almost too beautiful for words, and would make for some really great photos for the newspapers too… Raj?'

Raj was nodding thoughtfully as he pictured the scene. 'Yes, I like it. The palace is unique. It's very recognizable. No-one could be in any doubt that it's Tigeropolis. Great suggestion Matti.'

Matti smiled triumphantly, pleased that she had come up with the solution, and threw a rather self-satisfied look in the direction of her silly little brother.

'Cubs,' began Raj wistfully, 'did I ever tell you how your Uncle VJ and I spent much of our youth trying to avoid ending up permanently at the palace – as a stuffed exhibit mounted on the dining room wall? The day I came across the Maharaja on the road to Lis was quite a tale, I can tell you.'

Tala groaned. He had so many stories, and each time he told them, the more embellished and fantastical they became. She must have heard the one about the near fatal encounter with the Maharaja a hundred times.

One day, Raj had been walking along the forest track when he turned a corner and came face-to-face with the

Maharaja on elephant-back, fully armed, blunderbuss at the ready and only a whisker away. For some reason or other, the Maharaja had not immediately noticed Raj. But, in any event, it seemed there was no easy escape: on either side of the road there was a high chain-link fence. With no place to hide, he was trapped.

Raj's quick thinking saved the day. There were some old advertising hoardings attached to the fence. Quick as a flash, Raj flattened himself up against one of them and, smiling broadly, pretended to be part of the scene. Raj was convinced that the Maharaja had stared straight at him; yet somehow he didn't realize what he was really looking at.

The Maharaja (and his elephant) went on their way, ignoring Raj still pressed up against the poster. Tala couldn't imagine how Raj got away with it: after all, what would a tiger possibly have to do with selling petrol? None of the tigers she knew could even drive!

'Now, Matti,' muttered Raj thoughtfully, scratching his chin, 'the old palace might well be the right idea… But the question is how do we get the forest guards to change their plans?'

Bittu jumped up. 'What's wrong with just going over there and telling them? I'm sure they'd love it and, after all, we're all on the same side and want to save the park, don't we?'

'Yes, well…' said Raj, rather wearily, 'in theory, you're right Bittu but, in practice, I'm not so sure the humans are quite ready to sit down and discuss their plans with us tigers.'

He continued, 'I think, at least for now, we're still better working at arm's length. After all, the guards have only just come to terms with the fact that we exist at all. If we went to them directly, it would just raise lots of awkward questions: why did we go away… where are we living… what football team do we support… have we had our inoculations..? and so on. Before you know it, they'd be asking about your school, and how good are your grades?'

At the mention of grades, Bittu decided it perhaps best to just keep quiet. Raj concluded, 'So let's just stick with the plan, and keep working behind the scenes.'

Tala agreed. 'OK, Raj, point taken… Now how do we get them to alter their plans? We only have a few days.'

They all stood about thinking intently.

'Mind control!' exclaimed Bittu, excitedly. 'I saw it on TV last night. *Dr Wu*. It's really cool. He used it when they were trying to stop a troupe of pygmy elephant zombie cyborgs from destroying the Death Moons of Zog.'

Matti sighed and rolled her eyes. 'It worked one-thousand-million-percent!' he said, convinced this was the answer they had all been looking for. 'We just need to creep up to the forest guards when they're having their afternoon nap,' he said, moving slowly across towards Matti, weaving his paws back and forth in front of her eyes, all the while saying…

You are sleepy. Sleepy. Very sleepy. Listen only to my voice and obey my command…

When you awaken you will believe that the palace is the answer to all your problems.

The palace… Remember: the old palace!

'It works a treat! Dr Wu uses it all the time, honestly.'

The others ignored him and Matti broke what was becoming a slightly embarrassed silence: 'Well… what if… no, it probably wouldn't work… no… sorry.'

'Go on Matti, what is it?' said Tala.

Matti folded her arms, 'It's probably too difficult'.

'No, go on', Tala urged.

'Well. I was thinking... perhaps Bittu is right. Well... not actually right, I'd never go that far, but he might be on to something. Perhaps we could suggest the idea to them... *subliminally*,' she said miming quotation marks in the air with her paws. 'But a bit more sensibly than all that *Dr Wu* stuff.'

'Go on,' said Tala, intrigued.

She continued. 'Perhaps, tonight, we could secretly drop off a photo or two of the one of the grand parties they used to hold every summer at the palace. You know, the Maharaja in his diamond-encrusted turban, the servants in scarlet tunics and immaculate white cotton gloves, serving drinks and canapés from silver trays.

'We could drop it by the doorway of the chowki hut... make it look accidental. Like it fell out a magazine. Then, when the forest guards arrive, they would pick

Summer Ball – Palace of Lis

up the photo, recognize the palace and immediately see it as the perfect spot for The Grand Opening, and rush off to change their plans accordingly. Surely even the guards couldn't fail to take such an obvious hint.'

So that's exactly what they did.

Early next morning, just before sunrise, Bittu rushed off through the forest to the chowki hut and laid out some nice glossy photos on the doormat. They had found some great photos in Raj's old pink suitcase, including ones of the Lis Palace *durbahs* that were famous back in the old days. Back then, the Maharaja's family was one of the wealthiest in Northern India, and the most sought-after invitation of the year was to the Lis durbah. All the neighbouring maharajas were there along with the *nawabs*, the *nizams* and the *chhatrapatis*. Everyone had to make sure they had an invitation to the event of the year.

Bejewelled guests walked up a red carpet, flanked by the Maharaja's personal bodyguard: the Royal Lis Amber Cavalry. Resplendent in their bright yellow tunics and blue turbans, each held a razor-sharp curved *talwar* in salute. In the background, a fleet of Rolls Royce queued for at least a kilometre down a torch-lit driveway. Bittu's favourite photo showed guests tucking into a sumptuous buffet in the now ruined Crystal Conservatory with its stunning glass fountains.

It all stopped with The War, but the memory of the glamorous Lis durbahs lived on. There was no denying it: Lis Palace had once been a venue worthy of the most prestigious of occasions. The park authorities would be mad not to appreciate the potential to use it for such a high profile event as the reopening of Tigeropolis.

Having dropped off the photos, Bittu went back to the edge of clearing, hid in the long grass, watching and waiting excitedly.

Just as the sun began to fill the clearing with the first shafts of sunlight, he saw both forest guards arriving for their day's work. And, as if by magic, the younger one seemed to immediately take the bait. Just as Matti had predicted, he bent down, picked up the photographs, looked at them very closely for a good few seconds and then showed them to Mr Mistry.

Next thing, they were talking animatedly, pointing at the photographs and laughing. *'Result!'* thought Bittu, convinced he detected a knowing little smile flash between the two guards: the sort of look people give one another if they suddenly have a bright idea they just know their boss is going to love.

But Bittu's excitement was short lived. Once inside the hut, Akash had simply dropped the pictures into the paper-recycling bin next to his desk and got on with organizing his pens and pencils. Mr Mistry meanwhile walked across to the little side table and put the kettle on. It seemed that the photos had simply reminded them of the need to organize the parking.

'Anyone got a Plan B?' asked a dejected Raj a little later when hearing the news.

Plan B didn't go much better. It was Tala's suggestion initially. She photographed Raj and the cubs smiling sweetly and sitting among the best of the palace ruins. She then had some nice glossy A4 colour copies printed up and delivered anonymously to the hut in a big brown envelope with *'Party Photos – Do Not Bend'* printed clearly on the outside. She even added helpful little hand-written captions at the bottom of each photo as a further prompt:

Lis is More – Tigeropolis Tigers Enjoy Palace Home

Lis is a Palace for me

But, once again, the two guards just didn't pick up the hint. This time, they stuck a few of the pictures up on the wall, and turned back to making themselves another cuppa.

Back at the cave, the tigers sat down rather despondently to think again.

'Just where do they get the staff?!' said Raj, shaking his head in despair. 'Where, oh where?'

'What are we going to have to do before they get the message?' Tala added, exasperated.

It was Raj who decided that they needed a more direct approach. That night he sent Bittu back to the chowki hut to slip one final message under the door.

Next morning, as usual, Akash picked up the morning's mail from the mat. Half-hidden under the usual circulars for takeaway chapati delivery services and half-price solar-powered air-conditioning systems, was a large embossed gold-edged envelope, addressed rather ambiguously to *'The Officer in Charge'*.

He looked at the envelope a little intrigued by it all.

'In charge of what?' he thought to himself. He always felt a bit left out when all the mail came addressed to Forest Officer Mistry. This envelope, however, was clearly ambiguous, after all, he was in charge of the teacups and always did the washing-up. So he went ahead and opened it, scanned it quickly and smiled to himself.

It read:

You are Personally Invited to.........

The Tigeropolis Grand Chocolate Cake Tasting Challenge

To be Held at The Old Maharaja's Palace, Tigeropolis.

Today at 11.00h

Admit One Only

PS – Strictly Personal & Confidential – Tell No-one!

An invitation to a Chocolate Cake Challenge, thought Akash. What joy!

This was clearly an opportunity not to be missed. Akash quickly looked up to see where his colleague was, and whether he'd been noticed opening the envelope.

Luckily, Mr Mistry was focused on other things, and was already halfway across the office, preparing to make them both the day's first cup of tea. Akash knew that junior forest guards such as himself didn't normally get gold-embossed invitations (especially not to exclusive chocolate-themed events such as this), so he would have to be very careful how he handled things. He didn't want his more senior colleague taking over the invitation and going instead. After all, it was a *chocolate tasting*, and *he* was the expert: not Mr Mistry.

The organizers would surely be expecting someone that could appreciate, say, the difference between Mayan Chocolate Fudge and Ghanaian Chocolate Paste, or the subtle comparison between hand-rolled 81% Maya Smooth and machine-mixed 83% Ecuadorian Super Silk. No question about it: it had to be him.

And, he further rationalized to himself, he would actually be doing Mr Mistry a favour. Yes, he thought, it just wouldn't be right to embarrass a man of Mr Mistry's calibre by exposing him to such a specialist challenge as chocolate tasting: this was best left to experts such as himself. Noting that Mr Mistry was now busy with the teacups, he quietly slipped the invitation into his back pocket.

It was all going just as Raj had planned. Raj knew Mr

Mistry was far too wise to fall for the little ruse he was planning: he needed the younger guard to come, and to come on his own. He had rightly calculated the younger guard couldn't resist the lure of tasting the ultimate chocolate cake and, in his excitement, he would put to one side any suspicions about unexpected invitations. Just as importantly, Raj knew the young man's fear that his senior officer might take over such a valuable invitation would mean that he would also keep it quiet.

It had taken a while, but now things finally seemed to be falling into place as, sure enough, come 10.30am, Akash got up to go out, without mentioning the gold-embossed invitation or the tasting. He simply told his colleague that he had a couple of 'official duties' to do (after all, if a gold-edged invitation wasn't official, he didn't know what was).

As he left the hut, he casually mentioned that he might check the levels in the waterholes up by the old palace so, if it was alright with Mr Mistry, he would he take the jeep.

Forest Officer Mistry was vaguely puzzled by Akash's sudden enthusiasm for work (not something that happened every day) but, then again, not having to check the waterholes himself was one less thing for him to do… so why not let him take the jeep. And, of course, a little peace and quiet wouldn't go amiss either.

As Akash got into the jeep, he shouted back that he expected to return in about three hours. Typical, thought Mr Mistry: just in time for a late lunch.

Twenty minutes later, Akash turned off the highway that ran back to the village, and started along the rutted, overgrown track that led up to the courtyard in front of the old palace.

It was a bumpy track, but he drove along it quickly as he didn't want to be late. He passed the boarded-up buildings of what had once been the Maharaja's personal railway station and crossed the crumbling bridge over the Delbai & North Western Railway. Soon, he reached the courtyard in front of the palace. Even now, fifteen years after it had been abandoned, Lis Palace was still magnificent. It had easily been the grandest building in the whole state.

In its heyday, Lis Palace employed a house staff of over

a hundred, and at least as many again to look after the grounds. The Maharaja had a fleet of twenty cars and nearly as many elephants. The interior was decorated with white and black marble, inlaid with semi-precious stones in complex geometric designs.

At one time, the palace had contained some of India's finest Mughal treasures, along with gifts and antiques brought back from the Maharaja's many trips abroad. In pride of place had been the souvenir tea towel from Queen Elizabeth's Silver Jubilee, which the Maharaja had brought back from his first visit to London.

The palace had hosted kings and queens, two U.S. presidents and three foreign prime ministers. Famous celebrities, including Hollywood and Bollywood legends, flocked to the regular weekend house parties and, for three months one summer, the palace had hosted the entire film crew of Ritchie Battenberg's epic story of a chocolate dynasty, *Candi*.

As he approached the impressive façade, now overgrown with vegetation, Akash could still make out the beautiful pink-red sandstone of the Mughal-style building and its characteristic domed towers at each corner. The building rose to form a sort of fan-shaped frontage: just two storeys high at each end, but fully seven storeys high in the centre.

Looking from the courtyard, it seemed to be entirely formed of windows, each window etched out using elaborate stone tracery. There was one window for every day of the year, each with its own intricately carved, half-moon, stone balcony. At ground level, and plum in the centre, were three arched doorways; the central doorway nearly twice the height of the others. This was The Gate of Sublime Tranquillity. Only the Maharaja and his closest family had been allowed to use this centre door, on pain of death.

The Maharaja had loved his palace. It had been built by his great, great, great grandfather: The First Rawat Maharaja of Lis, Salaman the Bad. But now, two-hundred years later, it lay abandoned. It was just too costly to run: the window-cleaning bill alone came to one-hundred rupees per window every two weeks. Add in the bills for heating and lighting, the servants' wages, taxes, running costs for his three Rolls Royces, plus the tons of fresh palm fronds and weekly lilac water baths needed for his ten war elephants, and it had been obvious to everyone that the Maharaja could no longer afford to live there. So, somewhat reluctantly, the family had moved out to a more practical, newly built, four-bedroom semi-detached house at the edge of Lis. It also had a double garage: just big enough for one Rolls Royce and a small elephant.

That was fifteen years ago, and over the years the old palace had become a bit of a ruin. But it still held a certain magic, especially when viewed in the late evening sun, and set against a perfect, cloudless blue sky.

People said that if you half-squinted at the building just before sunset, from the little bridge that crossed the shimmering waters of the River Lis, you could almost still see the old Maharaja, with his long retinue of servants following on behind. The sight of elaborately decorated elephants tramping home from an exhausting (and usually fruitless) tiger hunt deep in the forest had been part of the pattern of life at Lis.

Twice a year, a truly spectacular event really drew the crowds when the Maharaja set out to visit one of the other nearby Princely States. The whole village would turn out to watch the procession. All ten war elephants, in full ceremonial armour, led the Maharaja's state carriage, accompanied by colourfully dressed musicians, bearers, bodyguards and other servants walking on behind.

But that was then. More recently, local villagers had been reluctant to come near at all. As the palace had become more and more overgrown, stories began to circulate of strange, unexplained happenings. Some believed that Salaman the Bad's eldest son, Salaman the Quite Naughty, haunted the ruins.

Salaman had been immensely proud of Lis and had the harem remodelled to a design similar to that used in the Akbar Palace in Agra. Legend held that he was crushed to death when he tripped and fell in front of an elephant, just as it was settling down to rest for the night. Locals told stories of how Salaman's squashed and flattened ghostly spirit could slip under any door.

Reputedly, on nights with a full moon, he could be heard rattling his jewelled scimitar against the windows; bewailing the dilapidated state of his father's magnificent creation, warning about the dangers of walking too close to elephants, and cursing his descendants for moving out to the suburbs.

Akash knew all about the curse. Everyone in Lis knew the story, but he had always dismissed it as an old wives' tale. He certainly had no thought of it as he pulled up in front of the palace. He was far more interested in thoughts of Ecuadorian Silk chocolate delicately melting in his mouth. Or perhaps some Mayan Chocolate Fudge. Mmmmmmmmmn.

He got out of the jeep, just in front of the central arched doorways. Despite his dismissal of the legends, he still quite deliberately ensured he went through the right-hand, smaller arch (the Citizen Gate), leaving the Grand Central Archway firmly closed, as befitted the private entrance of the Maharaja.

He was looking forward to the tasting.

CHAPTER I – The Invitation

Chapter 2 – The Tasting

Akash was standing in the cavernous Outer Grand Hall. It had once been a room to impress, but the furniture and embroidered carpets were long gone and the paint was now peeling from its ornate ceiling. He checked his watch: it was 11am. He was there exactly on time. But there was absolutely nobody around, and no obvious sign of activity.

He looked around in the half-light, as his eyes adjusted to the gloom. There, at the far side of the hall, he could just make out a small hand-painted sign stuck somewhat haphazardly onto a little wooden post. It said: **TASTING THIS WAY.** He followed the instruction and walked through a second doorway, which in turn opened out onto the palace's magnificent interior courtyard.

Stepping into the courtyard, he was met with an almost blinding glare, reflected off white marble floor tiles. Quickly retreating back into the shade, he could see the courtyard was neatly divided into four equal parts. Each quadrant contained an identical ornamental pond, each with its own cast-iron fountain in the shape of a leaping dolphin.

Surprisingly, given the building had been abandoned years earlier, cold, clear water still burbled freely from each dolphin's mouth. Even more surprisingly, each pond was home to a number of beautiful, well-fed golden carp, swimming aimlessly around under carpets of water lilies. But, apart from the fish, he could see no obvious signs of life. All those ghostly tales of Salaman, so readily dismissed before, had now suddenly started to make him feel a little bit uneasy.

Cloisters ran all around the courtyard. Above them was a myriad of small windows, each covered with carved lattice-work screens, designed to let air in and keep prying eyes out. They also had the added benefit of shielding those inside from the fierce heat and dazzling light of the noonday sun.

As a child, he had once been on a tour of the palace, so he knew roughly where he was. The area to the right had been the Audience Pavilions where villagers would present petitions to the Maharaja, and where feasts were held on special days. Immediately behind the Pavilions were the Maharaja's private apartments. The whole of the left-hand side of the courtyard was dominated by the harem. At the far side were the guardrooms, the kitchens and the staff quarters.

He tried some doors but they were locked: perhaps that was just as well. Fifty years earlier, for someone not of the royal household to be discovered trying to enter the Maharaja's inner sanctum would have meant certain death. Perhaps, he thought to himself, even now, with images of Salaman fresh in his mind, it was better not to push his luck…

'Hello..?' he called out hesitantly, looking around for clues as to what to do next… or at least for some signs of cake.

'Hello?' he asked again, a bit more firmly.

'Is anyone there?'

There was no reply.

It was only then that he noticed something half-hidden in the shade across the courtyard. It was a white porcelain plate, sitting on the edge of one of the lily ponds, with two large wedges of chocolate cake, each decorated with a crouching tiger figurine. The butter icing from the middle was already gently melting in the heat; slowly oozing out across the plate.

He went over to take a closer look. At the side of the plate was a small hand-written label in shaky writing, as though the person writing it had difficulty holding a pen.

TRY ME, the label beckoned.

Next to it, there was a scorecard with a little pencil, attached with string, with spaces for marks out of ten in each of four categories: Moistness, Sponginess, Chocolatiness and Presentation.

All most peculiar, but at least he knew now he must be at the right place: they at least had cake. He still didn't quite understand what was going on, and hesitated for a moment, unsure what to do next.

But the warm,
floury, chocolatey smell
wafting up towards him was
just too tempting. He put any
worries to one side, reached out for the
nearest piece of cake, and took a bite out of the
rich, delicious wedge.

'Mmmmmmmn,' he said lost in the deliciousness of the
moment, 'Perfection.'

He was just savouring the flavour of what he knew to be Ecuadorian Silk (and contemplating whether it was quite worth eight out of ten), when, suddenly, a voice boomed out above him, from somewhere in the shadows…

'Who dares to enter the House of Lis?'

Akash froze. Where on earth had the voice come from? He spun around, half-eaten cake still in hand. Nothing. No-one. He was unquestionably alone.

'Answer!', the voice demanded. **'Who dares enter the House of Lis?'**

'I… I'm, I'm F-fff-orest Officer Akash,' he said trembling, and trying to sound as official as he possibly could. And then he added, 'I mean… A-aa-cting Forest Officer A-aa-kash,' realizing he'd better be careful what he said, just in case Mr Mistry found out.

'Acting Forest Officer Akash-sh-sh-sh-sh?' the voice boomed back, reverberating around the courtyard.

'Ye-ye… yes,' Akash stammered.

The voice boomed out again, '**I have one question. Answer truthfully, as your very life may depend on it.**'

'Yes, sir... I will... I... I'm ready,' he said uneasily, finally putting down the half-eaten piece of chocolate cake and still trying to determine exactly where the voice was coming from.

'**Is it true: that the tigers have returned to Tigeropolis?**' asked the voice. As Raj spoke these words, he turned to Bittu and Matti, who were beside him next to the shuttered window, and winked. The three of them were standing at a balcony in the harem, looking down on Akash in the courtyard below. The intricately carved shutters completely covered the window, so they could see out, but no-one could see in. Raj was using an old megaphone to amplify and partly distort his voice. He had kept it as a souvenir from the days when he coxed the army boat crew, and it was finally being put to good use.

'Oh, yes sir, it's true: the tigers are back,' said Akash, somewhat regaining his composure. He had worried the question might have been a bit harder.

Raj was pleased. From Akash's quick response, it was

clear the forest officer was completely taken in. It was all going perfectly to plan.

'**Wonderful news, we must rejoice!**' boomed Raj, pausing for a moment for effect before going on, '**It is written in the Great Mugatabala of Lis that such a homecoming is to be welcomed a-thousand-fold, and with great celebration.**'

With Matti and Bittu giggling at his side, Raj was struggling to keep to his script. '**Forest Officer,**' he continued, '**the fortunes of Lis can only be restored if the tigers' return is embraced by the whole village and marked by a great and wonderful festival. The palace must reverberate to the sound of great joy and merry-making.**'

'But… but… the Maharaja has moved out, the palace is empty… there's no-one here to do the celebrating,' said Akash awkwardly.

'Mere detail,' the voice boomed. '**It is written and so it shall be. Excuses are not an option. Ignoring the prophecy spells dooooom!**'

'Oh, yes sir,' said Akash nervously, not least because he was somewhat unsure of what the Great Mugatabala of Lis actually was, but didn't think it quite the time or place to admit it. He certainly hoped it had nothing to do with Salaman the Bad.

The thunderous voice continued: **'This is what the Mugatabala commands! The palace must reawaken to welcome the return of the tiger. Order up the musicians, the poets and the dancers.'**

'Er, um… well… actually,' said Akash, 'we were thinking of something a little smaller… something… um, near the old forest rest-house, and… '

'**Enough!**' the disembodied voice cut him off mid-sentence. '**Do not defy the prophecy. Ensure the deed is done… and done well. The consequences of failure are not to be considered Mr Akash**-kashhhh-assshhh-shhhh.'

Akash's name echoed all around the empty courtyard.

Then silence.

(Silence, that is, except for a little burp from a goldfish that had just eaten a cake crumb Akash had knocked into the water).

'Ah, y-y-yes sir… yes indeed sir,' said Akash, surprised to find himself agreeing so readily to fulfil a command that a) he didn't fully understand, b) came from a disembodied voice he didn't recognize and c) was quoting from a book he had never heard of. Nevertheless, under the somewhat spooky circumstances, he certainly thought it a wise thing to do.

Finally, summoning up all his courage, Akash ventured, 'May I… may I ask one thing?

'**One question,**' answered Raj.

'Who exactly are you?'

'**Who am I..?! You dare to ask who I am..? People have been thrown to the crocodiles for less! I am the Great Guiding Spirit of Lis. Since the earliest days, my spirit, the Spirit of The Tiger, has guided the fortunes of the Palace of Lis… and indeed the whole of Tigeropolis,**' said Raj, now fully enjoying his role.

But, even as he spoke, he had to ignore yet more stifled giggles from Bittu and Matti. Raj glared in their direction.

He turned back to the megaphone and started speaking even more forcefully, this time leaving no room for compromise,

'**Celebrate, or a Great Calamity will unfold. Do I make myself clear Acting Officer Akash… kashhhh-assshhh-shhhh?**'

With his name reverberating around the courtyard,

twice as loud as before, a rather rattled Akash stuttered a response,

'Oh… yes, yes… Great Guiding Spirit… I understand,' and added a plea, 'May I go now, please?'

The voice was not finished with him and boomed back, **'Remember Akash you are now bound by a sacred pledge. You have eaten of the Sacred Tiger Cakes of Lis. Your pledge is sealed until death!'**

Akash looked down at the melted cake lying half-eaten on the plate in front of him. A pang of regret went through him for his weakness in eating the mysterious mixture. What had he got himself into? Why had he been so greedy and so gullible? He could see now it was obviously a trap. Who knew what might befall him next?

Far above, Bittu smiled at the thought of the 'Sacred Tiger Cakes of Lis'. Where on Earth did Uncle Raj get these great ideas?

Raj again took up the megaphone.

'You must tell no-one of our conversation. Never. Ever.

'Do you understand?

'**My spirit cannot rest if my secret is shared beyond the Chosen Circle of Cake Eaters.**'

'Y-y-yes', responded Akash nervously as all the various demands stacked up. How was he going to get Forest Officer Mistry to embrace the idea of a major change to the plans? But somehow he had to. After all, he had eaten the cake: there was no way out.

'**One last thing…**' Raj boomed out. '**I will send you this sign, should I need to summon you. When you receive this sign you must come immediately.**' As the words died away, somewhere in the shadows, Bittu put his paw through a gap in the fretwork screen and let go a small piece of paper. It fluttered down and landed right in Akash's hand. He opened it to reveal a single inverted black pugmark.

Standing beside his uncle, Bittu couldn't suppress a small smile of self-satisfaction. He had been practicing all

morning to make sure the
paper would float down
to just the right spot.

Raj continued, '**And
should you need
to contact me,
you may use
this…**'

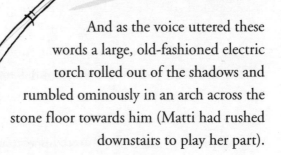

And as the voice uttered these
words a large, old-fashioned electric
torch rolled out of the shadows and
rumbled ominously in an arch across the
stone floor towards him (Matti had rushed
downstairs to play her part).

Akash put a foot out to stop it, bent down and
picked it up. As a torch, it was nothing special,
but stuck on the front glass was a rough-cut
silhouette of the same ominous
black pugmark.

'Flash the torch ten times against the southern palace wall, one hour before sunrise, then come to this spot and wait for my command (weekends and Bank Holidays excepted).'

'Understood. Now, please, may I please go now sir?' asked Akash plaintively.

'By all means go… you have much to do,' commanded the voice.

Akash turned to leave, but he was stopped by a loud call from the voice, 'But wait..!'

'Y-yes, what is it?' Akash said nervously, fearful of what extra demands might follow.

'Your cake. You've forgotten the rest of the chocolate cake. I had them baked specially… Oh, and you still need to complete the scorecard.'

'Oh-oh, yes, so I have… thank you sir, thank you,' said Akash bending down to pick up the form. He scribbled down some comments: *'Very nice cake, good texture, no soggy bottom, perfect flavour combination'*. As he turned to leave, clutching his remaining piece of cake, he mumbled, 'Yes, very nice indeed.'

Despite his ordeal, he once again had the presence of mind to use the smaller Citizens Gate. Who knows what terrible fate would await if he'd gone through the Gate of Sublime Tranquillity?

Akash ran as quickly as he could towards the jeep, not daring to look back.

He headed back to the guard post as fast as he could, checking his mirror every hundred yards or so, just to make sure he wasn't being followed. As he drove, he couldn't help thinking about the muffled noises he'd heard. If he hadn't known better, he would have sworn they were similar to the sounds he'd heard tiger cubs make when they were enjoying themselves. It had been altogether a rather unsettling morning.

When he finally got back, he was still agitated. Even

though he must have looked a bit spooked, Mr Mistry didn't seem to notice. With the words *tell no-one* and *you have been warned* ringing in his head, he said nothing of his encounter with the Guiding Spirit of Lis. Instead, he told Mr Mistry that everything was fine, and that after he had checked the waterholes, he had gone up to the old palace for a look around.

'You know Mr Mistry, it's a really… magical place,' said Akash as matter-of-factly as he could manage, 'When I was up there, it suddenly struck me that it might be just the right place for The Grand Opening. It's not like anywhere else in the park, and really says *Tigeropolis* to press and public alike. Something tells me it's the right place to celebrate it.'

Forest Officer Mistry thought for a moment. Why hadn't he thought of it before? He recalled the Forest Officer's Ball when he first arrived at Tigeropolis. The Maharaja had been patron of the organizing committee, and always offered the palace as a venue. Mr Mistry had even met his wife there. They had danced in the main courtyard under the stars. It had always been a special place to him. The more he thought of it, the more he liked the idea.

The Minister would also be impressed and it was bound to attract more publicity. 'Akash! That's a genius of an idea. It's perfect!' And, with that, he immediately set about speaking with all the suppliers, rearranging details and working out how best to ready the palace for such an event. By 4pm, he had even sent off an email to the Minister's office outlining his wonderful new idea.

CHAPTER 3 – THE GRAND OPENING

Oompa. Oompa. Oompa. Oompa. Boom.
Oompa. Oompa. Oompa. Oompa. Bang.
Oompa. Oompa.

Ting...... Ting......

TWANG!

The cacophony was finally at an end. Mr Mistry, somewhat relieved, took his fingers out of his ears and turned to the Minister's Private Secretary, Sadeep Welltenda.

Rather apprehensively he asked, 'Well, Mr Private Secretary Sir, what do you think?'

Sadeep, who had been sent to oversee preparations for the big day, took a deep breath and turned to face the assembled musicians. He gave a little applause; slightly less enthusiastically than Mr Mistry might have hoped for.

'Ladies and gentlemen,' he said, choosing his words

carefully, 'Thank you for allowing us to hear your rehearsals. I think I can say with all sincerity that your performance was quite... unbelievable. I am certain no other village in all of India has quite such an ensemble.'

He continued, 'I know I speak for everyone present when I say how much we are looking forward to your final performance of the day... Now, do *please* take a break from your preparations and have some well-deserved tea.'

As he watched the band shamble off, he turned to Mr Mistry and whispered, 'Luckily, the Minister will have to leave immediately after the speeches, so she won't actually have to hear them play.'

It was just after 9am, and they had all been working since sunrise. The preparations were now more-or-less complete: the old palace had been given a hasty makeover; the fallen stonework cleared away, the overgrown vegetation pruned back and a magnificent large white marquee erected in the courtyard. Baskets of freshly picked wild flowers hung from the balconies and a vast welcoming banner had been hung across the entrance.

Just in front of the main archway was a long raised platform. Placed at its centre was a large wooden table. The table itself was covered with the most brilliant white linen tablecloth, all edged with a red border and gold tassels. This was the prestigious top table, and it dominated the courtyard. It was reserved for the VIPs; the mayor, the village elders, the leader of the Lis Girl Guides troupe, the manager of the Tigeropolis United Football Club, the chair of the State Forestry Commission, the Maharaja and, of course, the guest of honour, the Minister herself.

Facing the top table were several smaller round tables with seats for ten guests. Each chair was covered in white cotton and tied at the back with giant white satin bows, as if at a wedding. In front of each seat was a silver place setting with a white orchid, two engraved crystal glasses and a souvenir *Tigeropolis Grand Opening* programme. Undeniably, it was a magnificent effort by all involved and clearly no expense had been spared in

celebrating the return of the tigers to Tigeropolis.

'Right, Mr Mistry,' said Sadeep looking down at his clipboard, 'Let's just go through this one last time. There must be no mistakes. The Minister expects things to go without a flaw. It's election year and that means, even more than usual, the press are on the lookout for any gaffs, or opportunities to snap unflattering photographs. My job requires the Minister to come out of this looking good. We must ensure everything goes like clockwork.

'So, taking it from the beginning… the Minister will arrive at twelve noon sharp. You will greet her on behalf of the Forest Department. You do this immediately after she steps out of her car. Akash's daughter Priti will curtsy and present her with flowers… Flowers..? Where are the flowers?'

One of the waiters dutifully held up a large bouquet.

'Great,' said Sadeep ticking off his checklist. He took a few steps inside the marquee and then pointed to a penned-off area away from the food. 'The press will be standing here and here,' he said pointing out each area very precisely. 'We mustn't let them wander off on their own. That way we can control exactly what photographs are taken and we can ensure that they will have a nice background with the old palace and all the flowers on display.

'Once Priti has presented the flowers, Mrs Banerjee will say a few words; introduce the Minister, praise her long-standing and tireless commitment to preserving Tigeropolis, and then refer to the Minister's unstinting work in support of all wildlife conservation more generally.'

He moved swiftly across to the platform and continued, 'The Minister will be standing here and will address the crowds… You are expecting crowds, aren't you Mr Mistry?

He went on without waiting for an answer. 'And then over here the girl guides will perform a first-aid demonstration, and the scouts will have a short country-dancing display. OK?'

Still not waiting for a response from Mr Mistry, who was, by now, looking somewhat overwhelmed, Sadeep went on, 'The Minister will then make a short speech, highlighting the glorious achievements of government over the last three years, decrying the policies of the previous incumbent and emphasizing her great pleasure at being personally involved in helping bring the tigers back to Tigeropolis etcetera, etcetera…'

Mr Mistry was bemused about the last part, as he could not actually remember anything the Minister had done to actually help bring the tigers back… but he was wise enough not to question Sadeep's statement and just nodded in agreement.

Sadeep went on, 'At that point, the Minister will finally declare the park *open*,' and as he said the word 'open', he snipped away at an imaginary ribbon with an extravagant flourish of his hand. 'The guests will then break into spontaneous applause. So do make sure they applaud Mr Mistry,' he added rather ominously, 'and with much enthusiasm.'

'Once the applause has died away, Mrs Patel will present the Minister with a suitable local souvenir of the occasion, as a token of the villagers' appreciation for all her hard work in reopening the park. I took the liberty of selecting a nice Karl Tigerfield scarf from the luxury mall in Delbai,' Sadeep said, holding up an exquisite silk black-and-orange scarf. 'Quite local enough, don't you agree,' he added, again more statement than question, before concluding: 'and then we can all finally sit down to lunch.'

Sadeep marked off a few more items on his checklist, and then turned back to Mr Mistry. 'Hopefully we can be away by 1.45pm… we wouldn't want to distract from the band's big performance, after all.' he added with a smile. 'Got all that Mr Mistry?'

'Yes, yes. Very good', said Forest Officer Mistry, smiling back and giving a little non-committal head wobble to try to hide the fact that he hadn't really been paying much attention to any of the detail. Hopefully Akash would get him through the day: with any luck he had been taking notes.

But Mr Mistry had a question. 'One thing, Mr Sadeep,' he said, 'Can you tell me at what point the Minister will want to go out tiger spotting? Mr Patel is keen to know when it's best to bring the jeep around.'

'Oh, I don't think that will be necessary: the Minister's not at all keen on dust and dirt. We just need to get a nice photograph of her smiling as she cuts the ribbon, a quick lunch, a wave and then we're off.'

'Mind you...' Sadeep stopped for a moment, looking thoughtful. 'On second thoughts...,' he smiled, 'with the election coming up... we're always on the lookout for good photo opportunities. They are usually the best way to get the Minister on national TV.

'People do love tigers... I wonder, could we improvise a bit... arrange for the Minister to cuddle up to a baby tiger? Perhaps even feed it?' he mused, getting more and more enthused at the prospect.

'Yes, something cute like that should get us prime coverage! Can you arrange that Mr Mistry?'

Before Mr Mistry had time to answer, Akash stepped in. Luckily, he had indeed been listening (and taking notes). He'd been following the pair around quietly in the background the whole time, just in case something tricky like this came up.

'Mr Sadeep, sir, if I may,' Akash interjected, 'I don't think that would be very wise at all, sir. Tiger cubs may look cute, but they are still wild animals, and I don't think they know what a *photo opportunity* is. Their teeth are quite big and sharp despite their size... one wrong move and the Minister might lose an arm. Now that might indeed make the news, but possibly not the kind of news you would have hoped for.'

'Oh,' said Sadeep, rather taken aback at the thought of the Minister walking around with one arm missing and blood spurting everywhere. He was beginning to appreciate that there might be a few differences between life out here in the jungle, and life back in their nice air-conditioned offices in Delbai.

With thoughts of photo opportunities put to one side and all the other arrangements now seemingly firmly in place, the three men trooped off for a well-earned rest. Only Mr Singh's chef was left, busily laying out the buffet and making final adjustments to the ice sculptures, humming along to a selection of famous Bollywood songs.

Two hours later, people began to arrive. In no time at all, Akash counted at least fifty guests, all dressed to the nines and enjoying the festivities. This was certainly the biggest event of the year in Tigeropolis.

Akash lent over and whispered to Mr Mistry, 'I see Mrs Banerjee didn't quite understand the invitation when it said 'decorations may be worn.' He chuckled, 'She obviously didn't realize it was referring to medals: not last year's Diwali glitter and trinkets.'

Mr Mistry grimaced at Akash, 'Shhhh, be quiet, she might hear!'

But Mrs Banerjee was too busy scanning the marquee and checking who was there to pay any attention to the forest guards. Within seconds, she spotted Sadeep and, ever keen to make an impression with officialdom from the big city, she immediately headed over to introduce herself.

Rather a self-important, slightly overweight, middle-aged lady, Mrs Banerjee was also unfortunately a little short-sighted. As she approached Sadeep, hand outstretched in forced greeting, she failed to notice a small wrinkle in the hastily laid carpet, and tripped. It was only a slight stumble, but it gave her a nasty jolt nonetheless and, even as she fought to retain her balance, she let out a rather loud, uncontrolled fart.

Pppppwwwwwwwp.

While Akash, Sadeep and Mr Mistry struggled to keep a straight face, Mrs Banerjee turned to glare at a passing waiter, delivering a withering stare of disgust, as if to imply that he were the real culprit for her unfortunate outburst.

Mr Singh came up to them, evidently in a happy mood. Bookings at his hotel were already on the rise, ever since the news of the tigers' return. He was even thinking he might need to employ a naturalist to take the guests around and explain all about the wildlife; the plants and trees, and the importance of tiger conservation.

'You know, Rahul,' Mr Singh said, putting his arm around Mr Mistry and taking him aside. 'You're shrewder than I thought. Knowing about all this tiger business, but cleverly keeping it all under wraps until election time. You knew the Minister couldn't resist coming to claim some credit for such a great news story. And, of course, now that she's involved, a good promotion in it for you too, I would think.

'Anyway... I've been meaning to ask you how many tigers

there are and, most importantly, where's the best place to see them? My driver will need to know all the details.'

Mr Mistry didn't quite know what to say. Of course, the truth was he hadn't actually seen any tigers since the news broke: in fact he hadn't seen any tigers for over ten years. Yes, it was all over the internet, but the stories were nothing to do with him, or even Akash. He hadn't a clue how the news had got out. But with Delbai so busy claiming the credit for themselves, no-one had actually stopped to question what was really going on. But now here he was being put on the spot. This was going to be a long day.

'Well, Mr Singh,' he paused, trying to think of something plausible to say. 'The fact is that tigers are difficult to predict. They might take some time to get used to people again. We might only see a few signs: pugmarks, scat and the like. An actual sighting... well, that might end up being something unusual and very special indeed.'

Mr Mistry wiped his brow a little nervously. He thought he had given a suitably vague answer, but noticed Mr Singh was now looking more than a little concerned. This was not what Mr Singh wanted to hear at all: he already had two groups of tourists booked to come and was expecting many more on the back of today's press coverage. They would want to see Tigers.

'But,' said Mr Mistry, seeing Mr Singh's reaction and realizing he needed to be a bit more encouraging, 'then again, of course, over time... possibly quite a short time... we can expect the tigers to get more used to humans and when that happens... well, sightings should be a great deal more frequent; at least I would definitely think so... wouldn't you?'

He was beginning to realize just how difficult this was all going to be. It was clear everyone in the village had ever-increasing expectations of what it all meant in terms of jobs and visitors. He could see now that this could all go horribly wrong. What if the tigers weren't there permanently at all? What if they were to move on, or worse, been poached? What would happen then?

He was already beginning to imagine the stream of angry communications from HQ, demanding answers as to why it had all gone wrong. He could picture the hoards of tourists, angry fists thumping against the chowki hut door, demanding their money back, while the villagers cursed his management of the park and their loss of livelihood.

Life had been so much easier when there were no tigers in his tiger park; when no-one had ever heard of Tigeropolis. Oh, how he longed for the simple quiet life when the most daunting task of the day was dreaming up new excuses for yet another 'nil return' on the monthly tiger sightings report.

Suddenly, his train of thought was interrupted by the noise of sirens blaring out, as two big black limousines, both with blacked-out windows, swept into the courtyard, along with four police motorcycle outriders front and back.

'The Minister!' declared Sadeep, 'Places everyone!'

After much hugging, kissing and welcoming, the dignitaries began to take their places up on the platform with the Minister seated right in the centre.

Once everyone was seated in accordance with Sadeep's plan, Mrs Banerjee, having by now fully regained her composure, got ready to start proceedings. But just as she was about to get up, the Maharaja suddenly took over. He stood up and immediately launched into a long ramble about his father; how he would have been so pleased to see the old palace at the centre of things once more, and how wonderful it was that the tigers were back at Lis.

Sadeep fumed silently: this was not how he had planned it. After a few minutes, he looked down at his watch, as the Maharaja started on yet another of his tales of the old days. Sadeep's carefully choreographed plans seemed to be rapidly turning to dust.

Meanwhile, Akash, who was seated at a side table along with the local police and fire services representatives, was not focused on the proceedings at all. In fact, he was pondering a conversation he had had with the Maharaja a few minutes earlier whilst they all awaited the Minister's arrival.

After briefly complimenting the Maharaja on the magnificence of the old palace, he had dropped into the conversation (he thought, rather cleverly) a casual remark about the old superstitions he'd heard concerning the palace when he was young. He had gone on to ask whether the Maharaja thought the palace might have ever been haunted.

Without a moment's hesitation, the Maharaja had answered with an emphatic 'yes', insisting that, to his certain knowledge (and who would ever contradict a Maharaja), there were no fewer than three ghosts, each more terrible than the last.

The most frightening, according to the Maharaja, was the ghost of Emperor Shah Ja Jahan Jan's most powerful courtier, Viresh. He had been beheaded a few years after the palace had been built. Legend had it that he had being wrongly accused of treason by the head of the palace guard.

The Maharaja had gone on to say that although he had never seen the ghost himself, his own grandfather had often claimed to have seen a headless Viresh prowling the corridors of the harem looking for his severed head, all the while shaking his fists and swearing revenge against anyone in uniform for his wrongful execution. Viresh, it seemed, was also sometimes heard in the middle of the day barking orders to invisible courtiers and demanding that absolute obedience be paid to the famous Guiding Spirits of Lis.

This was not really the news Akash was hoping for. He'd rather hoped the Maharaja would have had nothing to do with stories of ghosts and hauntings, so that he could safely dismiss his recent encounter at the palace as some sort of a dream (or perhaps down to something he'd eaten), and that he could quickly forget all about it.

He was also all too aware that the Lis forest guards traced their heritage all the way back to the days of Shah Ja Jahan Jan, when they acted as the palace guard. Who knew whether the ghost of Viresh would hold him somehow personally responsible for what had befallen him all those years ago?

Trying to put all such thoughts of evil spirits out of his mind, he began instead to focus on the buffet lunch to come; the red lentil curry, the spicy parathas and, of course, Mr Singh's beautiful special potato and aubergine pancakes. As his thoughts drifted on to dessert, he noticed, out of the corner of his eye, an unusual bright glinting light coming from the very edge of the forest.

It was most odd. All that was out there were trees: rows and rows of trees. Even stranger, the glinting came and went. As though someone (or something) was signalling to him. Surely he wasn't being watched… was he? He mustn't let his imagination run wild. He turned to Pradeep, a policeman friend from the village, who was sitting next to him.

Could he see the glinting?

Pradeep dutifully turned to see what was bothering Akash, but for all that he scanned the edge of the forest he could see nothing. Pradeep shrugged, as if to say whatever it was has gone and signalled instead that they should both turn back to listen to the rest of the speeches. The Maharaja was still droning on, and Mrs Banerjee was desperately signally him to stop so that they could all get back on track and declare Tigeropolis open.

But Akash was deeply puzzled, especially when a minute or two later he caught another flash of light coming from exactly the same spot. What was going on? Could it be that the Great Guiding Spirit was checking up on him? No. He was getting to be paranoid. He told himself there must be another explanation. The last ten days or so had been quite an upheaval.

If only he hadn't snuck off to the cake tasting. He had thought himself so clever rationalizing how the invitation might be meant for him. But ever since that day, their cosy little routine at the chowki hut had been turned upside down. It was incessant: requests from Delbai for this or that, reporters demanding photos or quotes, and all the locals forever pestering them for tickets for today. And now here he was in a tent outside the palace being spied on!

Then, looking across at the top table he realised, perhaps he was worrying for nothing. This wasn't for him.

It would be for the Minister. It would be something to do with her security team. You saw it all the time in the movies: the Secret Service sealing the perimeter when a VIP made a visit to a remote location. That was it. Of course, it wouldn't just be the bulky conspicuous guys in dark suits and sunglasses, who seemed to scan the crowd incessantly from the side of the platform. There were bound to be other people outside, securing the outer perimeter.

Relieved by his explanation, he found himself giving a little involuntary wave in the direction of the glint, as if to say 'Hi, Good job you guys. It's OK, I'm with you. I'm a forest guard.' Finally beginning to relax, he settled back in his chair to listen to what the Minister had to say.

But, of course, it wasn't the Minister's security detail out in the forest: it was Raj. The tigers were at the edge of the tree line, half-hidden from view, observing what was going on. Raj had brought his old army binoculars to get a closer look. Even the slightest movement of his binoculars caught the sun, and it was this reflection that Akash could see flashing.

In fact, the family had been hanging around in the

undergrowth all morning, observing the comings and goings at the old palace. They had been fascinated by all the preparations: the band, the flowers, the number of people and servants who were gathering and, of course, the motorcade and outriders that had swept up the drive to deliver the Minister. They were really quite impressed. After all, it was all for them: *the Tigeropolis tigers.*

'It seems to be going rather well,' said Raj as he swivelled his binoculars round to look at the crowd in more detail, 'Even seem to have managed to get Delly Telly along to cover the launch. That's really good. Oh, and look Prime Time TV too! No doubt about it... we're famous.'

Matti and Bittu were not content with Raj's commentary, and were jostling with each other to determine who'd be next in line to take a look. 'Can I have a look Uncle? Please..?' asked Matti, rather impatiently, and desperate not to miss anything.

'Yes, of course, Matti,' said Raj kindly, handing over the binoculars. 'They adjust here. See? Now try and see if you can spot the Maharaja. He's the one with the white turban.'

Matti cried out, 'Got him! He's standing up and giving a speech. The lady next to him is yawning.'

'Sooo like his father,' said Raj laughing, 'and hopefully just as short-sighted when wielding a blunderbuss…'

Tala was amazed they had been able to set this all in motion. Such pomp and ceremony! And all with just a few photos uploaded to Tigerbook and Indigram. 'Just think what we could do if we were really trying,' she mused.

'Mum, Uncle,' said Matti, turning to the adults, 'I know you both said we should keep our distance, but it all looks such fun… can't we please get closer and join in a little bit… please, Please?'

'No… I don't think that would be a good idea at all,' said Uncle Raj firmly.

'We would just get in the way,' Tala added. 'Much better we stay here out of sight. Humans prefer it that way.'

'Awww, but Mum… that's not fair.' said Matti, disappointed not to be at the centre of things. 'Pleeeeeeease,' she added, pleading even more insistently.

As always, Bittu hadn't been paying much attention to what was being said. He was distracted by the sounds of cheering, and the fireworks that had been let off as the ribbon was being cut. Caught in the moment, he suddenly jumped up and over the bushes, crying out, 'This is so exciting! Come on Matti, let's give everyone a big tiger-sized welcome!' and he scampered out into the clearing, and off in the direction of the old palace.

As he went, he gave out his best ever,

'ROARRRRRR!'

Raj shouted at Bittu to come back *immediately*.

Fearing Bittu was not at all paying attention, he also gave out what he hoped was a commanding...

'RRRRRRROARRRRRRRRR!'

...as if to say 'get back here at once!' Bittu charged on regardless.

Tala looked round at Matti and tried to grab her by the tail, hoping to at least stop her from joining her brother, but Matti cleverly flicked her tail to one side, and slipped right out of her grasp. She too was gone in a flash.

'ROARRRRR! ROARRRRR!'

the two cubs roared excitedly as they charged on downhill towards the palace.

'Oh dear... oh dear...' muttered Tala. She didn't think this was going to turn out well at all.

ROAAAAR!

She cried out to Raj, 'Raj,
do something! Stop them!
I don't think anyone
down there will be
pleased at this at all.'
She began to break cover herself,
and rushed out in pursuit of her cubs.

Raj threw his paws up in despair. It had all being going so well.

Tala was certainly right about the likely reaction down at the palace. Bittu and Matti's sudden enthusiastic intervention was not quite as welcome as the cubs might have hoped. On hearing the roars, the guests had all abruptly stopped listening to the speeches and turned instead in the direction of the noise.

What they saw shook most of them to the core. In reality, it was just two over-excited, naughty and playful little tigers running expectantly towards them to join in the fun, with an embarrassed mum in hot pursuit, plus an old uncle roaring sternly in the background. But to those unaccustomed to such things what they saw was a troupe of marauding, dangerous, *wild tigers*, charging towards them at full speed.

In some confusion, they all rose to their feet, plates and glasses flying. This only added to the sense of panic. Scared and shouting for help, the guests ran out as fast as they could to seek safety. Most ran straight into the palace: in fact, most of them went straight through the forbidden Gate of Sublime Tranquillity, completely ignoring the polite *'For Maharajas Only'* notice hanging from the doorframe. Once inside, they immediately slammed the gate firmly shut behind them.

Only the poor sousaphone player was left outside. The rest of the band had lead the rush for safety, but no-one thought to give him the assistance required to climb out from inside the centre of his giant instrument. Trapped inside the coils of brass tubing, the best he could manage was a sort of lolloping, hobbling motion as he made his way in panic to the palace. However, with a giant horn over one shoulder, it was impossible to make it through even the largest doorway.

Try as he might, the instrument kept hitting the doorframe, repeatedly knocking him flying. In his panic, and with escape seemingly not an option, he decided his only option was to grimly face the rampaging beasts. He turned to face Matti and Bittu, closed his eyes, crossed his fingers… and blew as loud as he could on his instrument:

Ooooommmp-oooooommmp!

While he vainly hoped the loud blasts might frighten

off his attackers, to Bittu and Matti it simply added to the fun. Plates flying in the air, people running hither and thither, then disappearing behind bushes, boxes and doorways... and now a nice old gentleman making funny *ooooommmp* noises on the palace steps! What fun!

'Look!' Bittu shouted at Matti as they bounded toward the marquee, 'They've all run off! I think they must be playing hide and seek. Let's join in!'

But, before he could make another move, he felt his mother's paw on the scruff of his neck, and he was lifted clean off his feet. Tala might have been slow to react to the cub's sudden dash out into the clearing, but she still had plenty of speed in a chase when it came to it.

'Bittu!' said his mother sharply, slightly out of breath and clearly very displeased, 'And you Matti! You should know better. Just what do you two think you are playing at?' She went on sternly, 'Look! Look around you. You've frightened off all the poor guests *and* ruined their banquet.

'Goodness knows what they thought. One thing's for sure they certainly know now that young tigers have absolutely no manners!' she said angrily. 'I'm ashamed of you... both.

'And the way you were running... They probably thought that a wild beast must be chasing you. No wonder none of them wanted to get involved... apart from that brave young man over there with the musical instrument...' she said, pointing at the hapless sousaphone player still blowing away forlornly.

'Now get back to your uncle immediately, and no more nonsense.'

The two cubs rather sheepishly started to walk back to the spot at the edge of the clearing, where Raj was once more surveying the scene through his binoculars. No doubt about it: they had certainly made an impression.

'Now, Bittu and Matti,' said Raj trying to suppress a smile, 'Let that be a lesson to you: never attempt to join an event to which you have not been formally invited. It's terribly bad manners and, goodness knows, it's just bound to cause trouble.'

Truth be told, after he had got over his initial annoyance at the way the cubs had run off, Raj had really quite enjoyed the ensuing chaos; the food flying about, the scenes of mayhem as the Maharaja and all the other guests dashed from hideout to hideout, as they panicked at two little tiger cubs scampering towards them. This was much more fun than life in the deep forest.

Meanwhile, back at the palace, people were gradually sensing that the danger had passed. One by one they began to re-emerge from their various hiding places: heads popped out of laundry baskets and feet dangled down from trees. Guests gradually took up their places again in the marquee, dusted themselves off and began exchanging stories about their role in the excitement.

After a few minutes the village band congregated around the still-in-shock sousaphone player and attempted to strike up a jolly tune to reassure everyone that all was well, and that these things were just part of day-to-day life in a tiger sanctuary.

Behind the scenes, however, all was not going quite so well.

The Minister's security detail had reacted instantly to the perceived threat. At the very first growl, a well-rehearsed plan swung into action. Without a moment's hesitation they had scooped up the Minister, rushed her from the table, out of the marquee and straight into the apparent safety of the palace.

They then careered through an open doorway that led into a long-forgotten storeroom. There was no other exit.

Small as it was, the team leader made an executive decision that it was the most secure option available in the circumstances. And with that, he had ordered one guard to remain outside while he ushered everyone else inside, and locked the door behind him.

Still struggling to work out exactly what they were dealing with, instinct and adrenaline had taken over. Radio messages were garbled and all they could hear from outside were sounds of panic. When they heard another loud crash (the top table and all its glasses and crockery had gone flying), the officer in charge instinctively flung the Minister onto some sacks in the corner, while the security team piled on top, planning to act as some form of human shield should another bomb go off. Brave as this was, it also proved to be an error.

Earlier that day Mr Singh's staff had filled the room with supplies to service the banquet's on-site bakery. The force of four bulky adults flinging themselves (along with the Minister) onto what turned out to be flour sacks proved to have disastrous results. Instantly, the room was filled with the fine white powder and everything, and everybody, was caked in flour.

As the dust settled, the Minister and her team began coughing and spluttering as they patted themselves down. Some people might have seen the funny side of it, but this was not the Minister's way. People in the courtyard could distinctly make out a woman's voice seeking an explanation for the chaos that had just passed.

'Sadeep!' exclaimed the voice: '… a word please. Now!!!'

Twenty minutes later, a still rather floury Minister emerged. Professional to the last, she said a few words of encouragement and indicated that she was looking forward to the next time she was invited to the park. She picked up her bouquet and her Karl Tigerfield scarf with as much grace as she could muster, before dustily jumping back into her motorcade and speeding back to the city.

Sadeep turned to the Maharaja with a wry smile and said 'Well, I think that went as well as it could, I suppose.'

The assembled guests regrouped. With the Minister out of the way, they were determined not to let a little distraction like a group of marauding tigers ruin their big day. Mr Singh quickly got his staff organized, tables were put back in position, and the remaining crockery collected up, washed and places reset. Soon everyone was munching away happily at what remained of the feast.

'Well, well,' Mr Mistry said rather bemused by it all, 'what a day!'

Chapter 4 – Teething Troubles

The news that tigers had 'returned' to Tigeropolis started to spread. It led all the TV news bulletins that night, and was front page in the local press the next day.

Under the circumstances, and given the total chaos caused by Bittu and Matti's over-enthusiastic urge to be involved, the press reports were surprisingly positive.

The *Delbai Times* went with the headline:

After a Paws of 20 Years – They're Back!

The *Hindustan Moon* went with the shorter:

A Roaring Success!

Of course, the *Times of Poona* couldn't resist going with:

GRRRRRRRRRRRRREAT!

The favourable coverage owed much to the fact that none of the journalists who were covering the event wanted to admit that they had been first to run for cover, cowering behind the pot plants and diving into laundry baskets.

The Minister was even interviewed on television once she got back to Delbai, and was being praised as a role model for politicians worldwide. She was now being celebrated as a leader in conservation (with no mention of how just a few weeks earlier she had wanted the park bulldozed for a new road).

The publicity worked. People wanted to see Tigeropolis for themselves. Hotel owner Mr Singh was never off the telephone dealing with new bookings, and Mr Patel was busy making arrangements to bring in other jeeps to cope with the demand.

In the park, however, there were teething troubles. Raj had been immersed in the detail of production planning.

He had decided that the old temple would make an excellent spot for him to make his first public appearance, but he was also keen to add some dramatic tension to the scene. The monkeys were to wait in a little group of jamun trees near the ruins and, when they heard a vehicle approach, were to start making a series of alarm calls...

'A-a-a-a-a...' followed by 'Eee, eee, eee...'

...as though warning other animals of the approach of a dangerous predator, possibly a tiger. Raj knew that this screeching would get the jeep drivers to stop and alert their passengers to something exciting happening in the forest. The monkeys would then run backwards and forwards over the branches pointing excitedly towards the palace steps...

'Oo-oo-oo-oo... Eee, eee... Oo-oo-oo...'

...then, with any luck (and meticulous planning), the tourists would finally be able to see one of the beautiful Tigeropolis tigers (well, Raj), basking idly in the warm, slowly fading light of the setting sun.

In rehearsals, the monkeys were proving unreliable,

running off distractedly at the merest flash of silver paper (which they associated with someone opening sandwiches), or the smell of a freshly opened banana. They seemed unable to focus on the task in hand, or take the simplest direction. Try as they might, the monkeys kept missing their cue, distracted by some shiny trinket or other. Raj finally hit on the idea of a simple buzzer switch that he could activate by a single swish of his tail. After a few tests, the monkeys finally seemed to understand:

One buzz: Rehearse
Two buzzes: Standby
Three buzzes: Go

Raj also remembered Cousin Vinni's advice: tiger sightings should be kept to the last part of the game drive. So he needed to plan other attractions beyond just sambar deer (once you've seen one sambar, you've seen them all). It needed something a bit more… *dramatic*. He called a production meeting with the family.

'How about the elephants?' asked Matti, helpfully.

'Yes, thought of them', replied Raj, 'Trouble is, they're

not very dependable…
always forgetting.'

'Oh, yes. Pity,' said Matti, 'What about the crocodiles?'

Raj perked up at the idea 'You mean the 'muggers' at the creek, Matti? Yes, they can be quite spectacular…'

'What a wonderful idea!' said Bittu. 'The track near the chowki hut goes over the river at the old bridge, and there's a great viewing point up on the cliff. It would be great if we could get some of the tourists to go down for a swim. The crocs would love it too! SNAP! SNAP! SPLASH! SPLASH! It would be great fun, even if we have to let the tourists escape in the end.'

'Thank you Bittu, good idea,' Raj responded. 'Perhaps we'll do something along those lines but, rather than chewing through the tourists, perhaps I'll speak to Anshul and the stunt teams from Deer Devils. I'm sure they'll come up with a practical solution.'

Before they knew it, the big day was upon them: the public re-opening. There was much excitement. Dawn had just broken, but it was still very cold. The village band had turned up to mark the occasion but got themselves in a fankle, as they were still undoing their overcoats when the first tourists entered the park, and so their rendition of *Cry of the Tiger* on sitar, drums, trumpet and accordion would indeed have made any tiger listening feel like sobbing.

Once the tickets had been collected and the guides were onboard, the first tourist group rolled out into the park.

Such was the historic significance of the day, Mr Patel had decided he would personally drive the first tour; the fact that he had never actually driven before being brushed aside as a mere detail. After all, his jeep had been sold to him as 'automatic', so what could be easier?

Half-an-hour into their safari, they had driven past the peacocks, stopped to admire the wild elephants as they crashed through the forest (but at least they had remembered to turn up, confounding Raj's misgivings) and spent ten minutes trying to track wild boar around the man-made caves at the edge of the old forest.

They then drove up towards the lake with the old fort on the escarpment above and came to a halt when Mr Patel was able to point out a set of fresh pugmarks. A *perfect* set of pugmarks ran right across the road in front of them (almost *too* perfect, a skilled observer might say).

Apart from the fresh prints, there were also some conveniently placed claw marks scratched into a tree near the roadside. Mr Patel shushed the excitable tourists, and explained the need to listen intently for any indications that other animals might have spotted a tiger nearby. But there were no alarm calls from the surrounding wildlife to warn of a tiger skulking in the undergrowth. In fact, there was not a single sound to suggest they were near. Somewhat disappointed at the lack of a tiger sighting, the group pushed on and finally came to the cliff overlooking the river.

'Standby everyone', whispered Matti, speaking into her headset at her observation post on the far side of the river. She was very much in her element, and had learnt quickly from Anshul and Picca at Deer Devils. Organization, planning and timing – these were the real tricks of the trade.

'Hold it… hold it… await my signal', she said holding her right forepaw up in the air, while fixing her gaze on the cliff edge. She saw three, four, five… now

six tourists, and finally Mr Patel, approaching the barrier and then looking down towards the river.

'Hold…' she was watching closely, and could see Mr Patel point out the muggers in the water below. The crocodiles were almost motionless, as they lay half-submerged in the clear shallow water, easy enough to see from the tourists' vantage point up on the cliff, but not so easy to see from the riverbank. Only the eyes and nostrils of the crocodiles were visible from the shore as they waited for any unwary animals to come down for what might turn out to be their last-ever drink.

From her observation point, Matti caught the glittering of sunlight off camera lenses, as photographs were taken from the viewpoint.

'Wait… on my count,' she whispered.

'…and… cue deer,' simultaneously dropping her paw to give a visual cue to anyone watching.

She allowed herself a slight smile of satisfaction as she watched the deer troop jauntily out of the jungle one-by-one, towards the sparkling, refreshing water.

'Muggers standby… on five…' whispered Matti into her headset.

There was a brief pause, the only sound the gently lapping waters and the slurp, slurp of the deer drinking peacefully.

It was an idyllic scene, although if you were close to the river's edge you might just have caught the sound of a young female tiger's voice somewhere in the bushes, softly counting down:

'Five… Four… Three… Two… One… and action!'

At that, all six muggers simultaneously sprang out of the water, mouths snapping furiously at the rapidly retreating sambar. Perfectly rehearsed, they all escaped back into the jungle. Or so it seemed: in fact, the expert eye might have detected that the sambars had already begun to turn by the time Matti's countdown reached two. The sambars were taking no chances: nice enough as the muggers had seemed at their first rehearsal, the sambars had no intention of becoming anyone's dinner.

'What a photograph!' exclaimed one of Mr Patel's

passengers, 'I was so lucky! I was just about to take a shot of the deer drinking, when the croc lunged forward… boy, how that sambar turned! I can't wait to see this properly on my laptop back at the lodge. What quick reactions those sambar have. Amazing… like they had a sixth sense warneing them of danger... how they escaped those giant snapping teeth I don't know…'

The tourists continued on their way, buoyed by the drama… but after nearly two hours of driving, there was still no sign of any tigers. Just as they were beginning to think this was not going to be their lucky morning, Mr Patel turned onto the Lis road. It was nearly 8am, and he knew they would soon need to be back at the lodge for breakfast. Suddenly, he noticed some monkeys high up in the jamun trees on the left, just beside the ruined lodge, at the edge of the track up to the temple.

A call of 'A-a-a-a!' suddenly rang out from the monkey group, to be answered by 'Oo-oo-oo!' from somewhere deeper in the forest. It seemed to be a monkey Morse Code. Alerted that there might be something interesting nearby, he turned his vehicle up the track.

'Hear that?' asked Mr Patel of his passengers, 'Alarm calls!' he said knowledgeably. 'The monkeys are the *eyes and ears* of the forest, they notice everything.'

'A-a-a-a!', the monkeys started up again, followed by another 'Oo-oo-oo!'

Mr Patel was getting excited. 'With that amount of calling we must be close to something… everybody pay attention. Keep your eyes peeled,' he said in a low whisper, 'but keep noise and movement down to an absolute minimum... we don't want to frighten off anything that might be out there...'

They drove on.

'Look!' he said excitedly. 'Over there... see?' he added, pointing across the courtyard. Heads turned to where he was pointing.

'A tiger!' he said triumphantly.

There, across the temple courtyard, was Raj, fully stretched out on the abandoned verandah, warming himself in the early morning sun. As he saw the jeep approach he sprang up as if startled, looking defiant. He put on his sternest expression, lowered his upper body as though getting ready to pounce and gave a perfect, low, menacing growl.

'Gggggggggrrrrrrrrrr...'

'Don't anybody move,' hissed Mr Patel loudly, somewhat concerned for everyone's safety. This was his first tiger sighting too, and he was unsure of what would actually happen. He stopped the vehicle as quietly as he could, and switched off the engine. All the while, his passengers, slightly shocked at actually coming face-to-face with a real live tiger, fumbled nervously for their phones and cameras. Make the wrong move and they ran the risk of having their head chewed off by a wild beast; on the other hand, it was a selfie opportunity not to be missed.

'**GRRRRRRRRR...**' continued Raj, a little louder and more purposefully, and now revealing his great sharp upper fangs.

'No sudden movements,' insisted the driver, 'Keep seated and... remember... please keep all arms and legs inside the vehicle: we don't want anyone to become lunch.'

Raj lay down again, smiling to himself as he heard the autofocus motors whir and beep, along with the click-click of shutter noises. When the initial commotion had died down, he waited a further few minutes before slowly getting up, turning away and walking off, stage left. He stopped at the edge of the temple, turned round, stared defiantly at the tourists and gave out one mighty last:

'ROARRRRRRR..!'

Finally, he turned away, and vanished into the undergrowth.

Bittu was watching through binoculars from the far side of the courtyard with his mother, who was applauding as quietly as she could. 'Just perfect, exactly as rehearsed!'

'Oh, oh... oh... my goodness, gracious me...' breathed one of the tourists, totally blown away by coming face-to-face with an angry tiger. 'It's just like on TV,' she continued, 'Wait 'til they see this back home, they just won't believe it.'

Mr Patel turned the jeep around and the group headed back to their hotel for some well-earned breakfast. They were all eagerly awaiting the opportunity to review their photos, and share the best on Tigerbook when the electricity finally came back on later that night.

CHAPTER 5 – THE PHOTOGRAPH

Mr Chowdry was used to the Maharaja's madcap schemes. He had been the Maharaja's personal assistant for over twenty years, and was used to the 'projects' that came to a sticky end when the fatal flaw in the Maharaja's logic finally emerged. Like the time when he'd decided to open up a white water rafting business on the river, just north of the village.

On their first (and only) trip, they'd forgotten about the giant crocodiles infesting the river, ready to ambush anything tasty that might be floating by. They would all have been killed if it hadn't been for a little group of deer that distracted the muggers at precisely the right moment.

Thankfully, because of the deer, only one of the crocodiles even bothered to come near them and even then showed only mild interest in the families in the little craft. It seemed one bite into the rubber of the raft was enough to tell the croc that baby deer were a better menu option, and off he swam to the riverbank to join his friends in the hunt. The next day, the Maharaja put the raft up for sale: the buyer didn't seem to mind the puncture marks on the side too much.

Then there was the time he decided they should invest in a franchise for portable outdoor ice rinks. The Maharaja had seen them on a trip to London one Christmas, lots of happy children enjoying themselves skating next to famous landmarks. There and then, he decided he should set them up all across India. The differences between a frosty December in London and the forty-degree average temperature back home didn't seem to occur to him. The ice rinks wouldn't freeze: instead of ice-skates, the customers needed flippers.

It was therefore no surprise to Mr Chowdry, as they sat down together for their regular morning meeting, to hear the Maharaja come up with yet another plan. Only this time, there seemed to be some actual logic in what was being proposed: the Maharaja wanted to convert the old palace into a hotel. With the tigers back in Tigeropolis, he was sure lots of tourists could be expected and some might well fancy the idea of a night or two staying in a famous palace. Even the Minister had wistfully remarked, as she stood beside him at The Grand Opening, that it was 'such a shame' that wonderful old buildings like these had fallen out of use.

The Maharaja himself had been excited to be back at the palace, seeing the old building thronged with people, just like the old days. He was sure people would love the Mughal architecture, and the memories of pomp and pageantry. He might even get the staff to dress up in the uniforms his own grandfather had designed: the silks, the gold braid, the solid silver buckles and buttons, topped off with diamond-encrusted ceremonial daggers. Of course, he'd have to do it at a fifth of the cost, but he was sure they could get something run up in the local tailors that would do the job.

As always, the Maharaja had quickly skipped over the detail and concentrated on the fun. It would be left to Mr Chowdry to actually make it work, though unfortunately he too knew next to nothing about running an international luxury hotel.

Mr Chowdry decided to contact his old friend, Gurminder, who ran the Tiger's Lair Palace Hotel at Ranthgarh for advice. With that settled in his mind, he indulged the Maharaja in his talk of raiding the old attics for some furniture, the suitability of The Crystal

Room, with its ten full sized chandeliers and mirrored gilt walls as a dining room, and whether the old Elephant Washing Parlour and the Tusk Polishing Salon next door would make a perfect swimming pool and spa. They even wondered if they should reinstate the porcupine maze.

They would also need to think of planning permissions, hygiene regulations, rules about waste management, energy efficiency and water conservation. The irony was that Tigeropolis itself had really only survived as a nature reserve because it had once been the palace's own private hunting grounds, and consequently outside the scope of any Forest Department regulation.

Drawings, lists and budgets were scribbled down as the ideas flowed, and yet, as the meeting progressed, for all his apparent enthusiasm, Mr Chowdry became more and more aware that the Maharaja was not fully concentrating. He kept glancing down at the weekly newspaper lying on the table. Its front-page splash headline was all about The Grand Opening. Just below the photograph of the Minister cutting the ribbon was another photograph of a tiger prowling around on the top of the steps at the old temple.

It was one of the photos Bittu and Matti had uploaded when first announcing to the world that tigers were back at Tigeropolis. The Maharaja kept looking at the image. And he couldn't help thinking the tiger was somehow familiar.

The thought continued to trouble him long after the meeting with Mr Chowdry ended. He sipped his tea, took a bite from the *Parle Me* biscuit he had in his hand and thought again. Where had he seen that tiger before..? It was really beginning to bother him.

About an hour later, he went purposefully to his study, climbed his library steps and reached up to take down a dusty old A4-sized box file. He brought it down, opened it up and took out his old photo albums. He flicked through pages and pages of faded photographs of garden parties, family trips to temples, and summer balls. Finally, he stopped at a picture taken on one of his regular (and mostly unsuccessful) tiger-hunting expeditions. This particular photo was shot as he was taking the traditional 4pm tiffin by his favourite shady spot near the River Lis.

He remembered the days vividly; the excitement of the chase, the possibility of outwitting of the prey, the promise of success (even though the pesky tigers usually evaded him), and his favourite part of all: the well-deserved tea and scones down by the river afterwards.

Picking up his eyeglass, he looked more closely at the photo. All things considered, it was a nice picture of him sitting having tea and smiling his best Maharaja smile. He'd originally intended to frame this photo and place it on the mantelpiece along with the rest of the main family photographs... but for some reason he had changed his mind. At first he hadn't noticed it, but his wife, the Maharani, had pointed it out.

In the background, poking out of the bushes bold-as-brass, was a full-grown tiger! Clearly neither the Maharaja, nor the chap taking the photograph, had the slightest inkling the tiger was there. Worse still, the tiger was cheekily waving both paws in the air and sticking out his tongue: *'Naa, naa-na, naa, na!'*

Nowadays, they'd call it photo-bombing, he thought, but back then it was just called bare-faced cheek!

The Maharaja had been furious when he saw the photograph. He'd been chasing the tiger around for three-hours, without success, and there it was: making fun of him. He was initially going to rip the photo up; but he was never one to let an insult go unchallenged, so he had filed the picture away for future reference… just in case. One day, he felt sure, he would get his revenge.

He picked up the phone, and dialled his old hunting friend Jamcor Bett. 'Jam? Maj here,' he said, using the old school nickname that had stuck for all these years.

'Remember that tiger I could never bag, the one with the handlebar whiskers? Well he's back… How about this time, with your help, we finally get him?'

'Are you sure..?' enquired Jamcor, 'That was a long while ago. Surely he'd be dead by now?'

'Quite certain it was him… stripes are a perfect match, no doubt about it: it's Raj,' he said bluntly. 'I saw him once, ten years back in Scotland, at the Royal Military Tattoo. He was leading the mass bands as mascot of the 52nd Indian Frontier Rifles.'

'Well, if you're sure..?' replied Jamcor, unconvinced.

The Maharaja put down the phone, took another look at the photo, and muttered, 'So, my little photo-bombing friend… it's been quite a while. But we'll see who has the last laugh now.'

CHAPTER 5 – The Photograph

Chapter 6 – The Souvenir Shop
and the Ashram

Matti was indignant 'Well, I think *Tiger's Breath* is a great name. It's so evocative. It's what we are all about.'

'Yes… but not for toothpaste,' said Raj. 'When people are cleaning their teeth they want something that suggests clean and fresh, something more like… I don't know… like… *Himalayan Ice.*'

They were all gathered together looking at glossy catalogues full of possible gift products from around the world. They'd decided they needed some interesting tiger-themed souvenirs for the Tigeropolis Souvenir Shop.

'Mugs and tea towels. They're always popular,' offered Raj.

'What about these?' said Bittu, pointing to a picture of a little snow globe in one of the catalogues. Inside the clear plastic dome, a model soldier was standing to attention at a sentry box in front of a picture of Buckingham Palace.

'Amal has one. He brought it to school last week,' he said. 'You turn them upside down and little snow flakes drop down out of the sky and slowly cover up the tiny model soldier trapped inside. We could have one with the old temple.'

'Yes,' interrupted Matti, 'We could have a little plastic Uncle Raj having his regular afternoon snooze in the sun! Ha-ha!' she said taking up the theme. 'And instead of snow, we could have Uncle Raj slowly being buried in layers and layers of dried-out teak leaves, with perhaps some sound effects thrown in. Lots of loud snorting and snoring!'

'That's quite enough of your cheek, thank you Matti,' said Tala firmly.

Raj harrumphed, keen to get back business.

Tala continued, 'Of course there's still the elephant dung paper... I liked that idea the minute Cousin Vinni mentioned it. Very popular, he said. And perhaps an ink stamp that makes pugmarks? I could see all the children having fun stamping tiger prints all over envelopes and jotters and things.'

Raj nodded, 'And we should have a line of greeting cards, with shots of us as a family on the front; just like the chief minister does at Holi. Most appropriate.'

'Oh, look!' shouted Matti, pointing at a page. 'We must

have pencils Uncle… with cute fluffy tiger heads on the end.'

'What about a homestay?' said Bittu, 'I bet people would love to have a sleepover here in the cave with us!'

'Homestays with *us?*' said Tala, 'you mean *LairBnB?* I don't know whether I like that idea Bittu… From what I've seen, tourists are always catching colds, coughing and wheezing all over the place. Goodness knows what we might catch from them! We'd need to see their inoculation certificates first… no, I don't like it at all. Remember what Vinni told us..? Keep tourists firmly in their place: in their jeep. Don't mix with the clients.'

She reflected for a moment and added, 'But what about having them stay at the old palace?'

Matti giggled: 'Oh yes… and they might want to be haunted by the Great Guiding Spirit of Lis, Uncle Raj? I'm sure they'd love a nightly appearance of you wandering along the corridors draped in an old bed sheet!'

Raj ignored his niece's insolence, 'Well, some great ideas there: well done. I think we deserve a treat for tea after all that hard work.' And with that he ambled off in search of some lentils.

Next day, Raj set about organizing things. It was quite handy that, along with the old typewriter he had salvaged from the village rubbish dump, he'd also picked up some discarded sheets of unused Forest Department official notepaper. Even better, it was from the time when Tigeropolis had been finally allocated an official postcode ('T1 G3R'). Having the postcode made ordering from suppliers so much easier.

Some days later a little red India Post van chugged up the dusty track to the chowki hut. A gawky young man got out and lumbered into the office. 'Forest Officer Mistry?' he enquired.

'Yes?' replied Mr Mistry, rather wearily, thinking the boy was probably bringing yet another packet of official forms the *babus* back in Delbai wanted completed. Sometimes his life seemed to be one endless mound of paperwork.

'Got twenty packages for you… sign here, please,' he said, proffering a rather grubby form on a clipboard, before offloading the large grey cardboard boxes. The postman got back in the van and tootled off, back into town.

Mr Mistry turned to Akash, 'What on Earth can these possibly be?'

They carefully opened each box and began to spread out the contents on the office floor.

Mr Mistry shrugged his shoulders, 'Would you believe it?' he complained. 'Look at all this stuff. Soooo typical of Delbai.'

He was surrounded by multiple piles of pencils, greetings cards, elephant dung notelets, tiger-stripe tea-towels, pugmark-patterned mugs and, most curious of all, several dozen small globe-like objects. Each had a little plastic tiger trapped inside, buried in what looked like crumpled-up bits of brown raffia paper.

RAJ'S TEMPLE TIGEROPOLIS

'No idea,' said Akash, 'but it looks fun,' picking up the globe. 'Look, you turn it upside down and little leaves float down to cover the tiger. It's on the temple steps. My kids will love it.'

'Who ordered all this rubbish?' said Mr Mistry, not convinced. 'Not a mention of any of this from HQ… and what do they expect us to do with it? We're forest guards, not shopkeepers!

'Don't they understand the constant dangers we face? Daily walking mile after mile on patrol in the searing heat, constantly on the look-out against sudden ambush from wild beasts?' As he contemplated the enormity of his role, he took a sip of tea and munched at the cookie Akash had brought in.

'Yes. Forest guards, not shopkeepers,' he reiterated, brushing the plastic packaging off the desk and rearranging the pugmarked mugs carefully in neat rows of different colours and sizes. 'No consideration… none at all… just no idea of the amount of work we do,' he muttered to himself, while carefully folding some of the souvenir tea towels and placing them neatly on a shelf.

Akash nodded sympathetically, all too familiar with Head Office never telling them anything and just dumping them with the next ill-thought-out 'bright idea' or mad scheme. 'Oh well, I suppose they know what they're doing,' he said, resigned to his fate. He walked over to make a nice place for the 'snow globes' right in the centre of the window ledge.

And so Tigeropolis, despite Mr Mistry's moans at HQ, found itself with its own little souvenir shop in the corner of the chowki hut. Little did they know that it would, one day, become famous the world over for its weirdly compelling *Tiger's Breath* toothpaste.

Over at the cave, Raj had been busy on another front too.

He had been in contact with his twin brother VJ. They hadn't been in touch for a while, but Raj thought it might be helpful to have another adult tiger in the park to cope with peak demand, and with Saturdays, Sundays and public holidays. He was also all too aware that Diwali was not that long away and the public would be out in droves. Picnics were something of a Diwali tradition in the area, so they could expect lots and lots of tourists.

Uncle VJ was a favourite relative for the cubs. He was a bit of a rebel, and very much the opposite of Uncle Raj. Uncle Raj liked his brother, but didn't always approve of his ways. Raj's military background meant he always wanted to be in control; always neat and tidy and always ready for the next task. In contrast, Uncle VJ had spent his youth deep in philosophy and music. It was Uncle VJ that had persuaded the family to go vegetarian. He had spent whole summers in an ashram, a mountain retreat beside a tributary of the Ganges, seeking enlightenment.

The ashram had been run by the revered mystic, Yoga Bearra: an elderly, grey-haired sloth bear. Like most sloth bears, he had an almost insatiable passion for honey. It seems he had taken up meditation after being badly stung by killer bees when hunting for honey in a rhododendron plantation halfway up the Hindu Kush, between Afghanistan and North Pakistan.

In excruciating pain, it took him two days to crawl back to get help and, legend has it, he only survived the intense pain by constantly repeating what was to become his mantra: *'Honey for tea, honey for me.'* For two years after the incident he said nothing else.

Many years later, VJ met the Yoga again when he was teaching in the hermit caves at Vultures Rest. He held the young VJ spellbound with his tales of travels through India and beyond, and how he opened an ashram on a mountain-top, looking down onto the Ganges. It was frequented by the rich and famous, including four young lads from Liverpool, who arrived at the ashram one summer long ago. It was a time of great social change, of rockets to the moon, and of new technologies and fast cars. But people also realized that there must also be a spiritual side to existence, and much more to life than acquiring the latest shiny toy.

These four lads happily spent weeks listening to the Guru, practising yoga at the rising and setting of the intense Indian sun and spinning cloth.

The lads became known to everyone around as 'The Flab Four', because of their insatiable appetite for *gulab jamun*. They quickly created a vibrant community around them, and it seemed they were destined for great things. They brought their friends along, including a bunch of web surfers from a teacher training college in the USA, who became known as 'The Teach Boys'. They so appreciated the simple diet offered up at the Ashram that they went on to write a song about the food: *Shouldn't it be Rice*.

In addition to meditation, Yoga Bearra had taught one of them the sitar. VJ often wondered what happened to all those boys.

'So you're really going through with this, Raj,' said VJ walking into the family cave as though he owned it. He carefully set down his rucksack and paisley-patterned sitar case, before making himself comfortable, cross-legged, by the open fire.

'Yes, absolutely,' said Raj, slightly annoyed by the arrival of his twin, even though he had instigated the visit. He liked VJ, but mainly when he wasn't actually there.

'So, let me get this clear,' said VJ, absent-mindedly playing with his marigold garland, 'You want me to open up the old meditation caves in the cliff at Vulture's Rest?'

'Yes VJ, I think it's just the thing,' replied Raj. 'People are very interested in spirituality now.'

'Do you really think so?' said VJ.

'Yes, brother, I thought your old cave would be a great attraction, what with all the famous people you used to commune with under the Guru', said Raj, with a mix of admiration and annoyance at having to acknowledge that his brother's activities all these years might actually have value for their plans.

'Well, if you say so… I'll think about it,' said VJ, somewhat non-committal, and worrying that this might all be too commercial for him. 'But before I decide, I'll need to contemplate what it might all mean for my spiritual path.' Saying that, he clasped his paws together in front of his chest and gazed silently into the distance.

After thirty seconds, VJ suddenly dropped his paws back to his sides and turned to the cubs. 'Bittu! Matti! How are you both? My, how you've grown… And how has your sitar practice been going? Are you keeping up with the practice pieces I left you with last time I came..?'

Being asked about sitar practice was the one downside of Uncle VJ's visit. While VJ was fun, somehow sitar practice always seemed to get in the way of football. Bittu nodded vaguely, hoping Uncle VJ wouldn't pursue his enquiries too far.

The Yogi had taught VJ the art of the sitar. He was now something of an expert, and quite in demand for concerts, weddings and bar mitzvahs. Whenever he appeared at the cave, he usually brought his sitar. 'Good,' said VJ, 'Now, before you give us a recital, cubs, let me demonstrate a riff that my old friend Ravi taught me…'

Bittu heaved a sigh of relief. He knew from experience that his uncle would get caught up in the music and would completely forget to ask them to play.

'It goes like this…' said VJ, picking up his instrument.

Doinnnnnnggggg, twirly-dinnnnnnggggg, pung pung pung, tling……etc

After twenty minutes of continuous playing, VJ stopped and turned to his brother.

'Brother, I have reflected on what my Guru would want at a time like this.

'I agree that Tigeropolis is too important to be left to the bulldozers. I believe the Guru sees this as the right and true path, and would agree that the next part of my journey is to help you all, and that I should re-open the caves of the Hermit Kingdom.'

Tala had just joined them. 'Oh, I'm so pleased to see you VJ. Great that you've come to help. But, I don't think it'll be quite as simple as Raj thinks. The cave complex is all blocked up. The Forest Department put up an iron fence years ago to keep souvenir hunters away… remember?'

Raj reacted quickly 'Oh yes, I'd forgotten that. We'll need the Forest Department's help to remove the gate.'

'Is that going to be possible?' said VJ.

'Hopefully,' mused Raj, 'we've certainly done well so far.'

Next afternoon, on the other side of the forest, Akash walked into the chowki hut, all hot and dusty after his regular patrol along the river. Casually, he put down the stout *lathi* stick he always carried when out on official business. It was a poor defence against an angry wild animal, but there you were, that was the Forest Dept for you. The department didn't believe in arming forest officers with guns, so instead they had issued them with a stick.

They had been doing so since the department was formed way back in 1865, and one thing Akash knew from experience was that, tigers or no tigers, they weren't going to change anything in a hurry.

As he sat down, he noticed a small piece of paper sitting right on top of the pile of reports he had been gradually working through the day before. It was a single piece of A5, crisply folded in half. He wasn't entirely sure, but he couldn't remember it being there before he went out.

Curious, he picked
it up and opened it
out. As he did so his
jaw dropped.

He stared open-mouthed.
There it was, right in the
middle of the sheet, a single,
unmistakable, upturned black pugmark:
just as he had been warned to expect.

What could it possibly mean? One thing he did
know was that the voice from the shadows had
been insistent: if he received a sign he had to go to
the palace immediately. He glanced quickly at his
watch. It was already nearly 3pm. It was an hour's walk
to the old palace. If he was to get there (and preferably
back) before sundown, he would need to leave now.

It took him slightly longer than he anticipated. The last
mile uphill had been a bit of a struggle. Perhaps, he
reflected, he ought to cut down on the chocolate cake,
as he was clearly not as fit as he had been when he left
school. The late afternoon sun bathed the palace in a
wonderful light that brought out the pinky-reds of the

sandstone and the ever-bluer sky, as he finally arrived.

He was more than a little apprehensive as he cautiously approached the gateway. He couldn't help but remember his conversation with the Maharaja at The Grand Opening. Three ghosts, each more terrible than the last, he had warned.

When Akash thought about this, his blood ran cold. Could he really have been talking to the ghost of this courtier earlier in the week? Could he still want revenge? Surely, as a ghostly spirit that seemed so well disposed towards tigers, he wouldn't hold any grudge against a mere forest guard like himself.

Trembling, and slightly sweaty from the exertion, Akash opened the entrance gate and walked slowly into the inner courtyard. Just as before, he heard a deep voice boom out.

'Akash, I am pleased to see you answered your summons.'

'Thank you, Great Guiding Spirit,' said Akash, now becoming slightly more used to speaking with a disembodied voice somewhere up there in the darkness. As he spoke, his eyes scanned the courtyard, desperate to catch a glimpse of something that would help him discover where the voice was coming from.

'**Progress has been swift since we last spoke. This is good. The Mugatabala also forecasts that with the tiger's return comes an opportunity for renewal. To allow this renewal, you must remove the gate that blocks the way to the Hermit Kingdom on Vulture's Rest,**' the voice commanded.

Akash was just about to ask what 'renewal' might mean when the voice boomed out again:

'**No questions, Akash, just obedience. I have spoken… Now go!**'

Then silence.

First thing next morning, Forest Officer Akash scrambled up the rocky path to Vulture's Rest, with a crowbar and some wire cutters. He reached the spot where ten hermit caves had been cut into the rock face over a thousand years earlier, and began to force open the iron gates.

Chapter 7 – Revenge

Bittu rushed excitedly up the temple steps, looking for Raj to tell him the news. He was just about to burst into Raj's favourite room when, from somewhere inside, he heard the familiar, deep bass chants...

'Oi anna coom... oi anna coom zeee.'

He knew exactly what that meant, and immediately slowed to a walking pace before peeking round the doorway and into the room.

'Oi anna coom... oi anna coom zeee,' the chant repeated, over and over again.

There in front of him, levitating ten centimeters off the ground, with his hind paws interlocked in a half-lotus position, was not his Uncle Raj, but Uncle VJ. Eyes shut, breathing deeply, his mind was focused on the chant.

'Oi anna coom... oi anna coom zeee.'

Bittu knew that, no matter how important his news,

it was going to have to wait until VJ had finished his meditation. Communing with his inner *chi* was of paramount importance to Uncle VJ. Nothing came before it. Nothing.

A minute or two later, the chant finished. Mind and body relaxed, VJ slowly unwound his legs, brought his giant paws down to the floor and finally released his claws. He sat back, still with his eyes closed, raised his front paws above his head and then brought them back to touch in a clasped position just below the chin. He then gave a little bow to signify the end of the meditation, and slowly stood up.

Yoga session over, he turned to acknowledge Bittu, and asked him what brought him to the old temple.

'Well,' said Bittu, 'you might not believe this, but I was coming home from football practice... we're playing the Ranthgarh Lions next week in The Cup... going to be a tight game... they're good... we're trying a new system, three upfront... anyway... I did really well, scored a hat-trick, even nutmegged Eashan... you know, the elephant that plays the sweeper role for the Parrots... he's always a second or two too slow, so it's always on for me to beat him with a dummy to either side...'

As he talked, Bittu acted out the movements, dancing past an imaginary Eashan, before finishing off with a kick at his imaginary ball and flinging his paws up in celebration: 'Goooaaal!' he exclaimed.

'Never mind all the *Match of the Day* analysis, Bittu: get to the point. What exactly is so amazing that you think I'd not believe it?'

'Well Uncle, as I said, I was just coming back from practice, and kicking my ball along in front of me. I must have kicked it a bit too hard, and it went under a bush. I think it was a bougainvillea – very sharp thorns. I had to crawl right under to try and get it back.

'So, there I am, under the bush, straining to reach my ball, when next thing, I hear a jeep going past. I looked up from under the bushes to see the Maharaja, and with him was… and this is the bit you won't believe… with him was Jamcor Bett!'

Bittu was aware that the name was one both his uncles knew only too well.

'Are you sure, Bittu?' said VJ, genuinely surprised.

'I thought he had retired to the seaside years ago,' continued his uncle, trying to look at ease in front of his nephew. The news was something he had been secretly dreading ever since he first heard mention of Raj's plan to publicly announce the tigers' return to Tigeropolis.

'Oh yes, it was him alright. I've seen all the documentaries about him on Delly Telly. I'd know him anywhere,' said Bittu proudly. 'Oh, and of course it helped that his jeep had *Jamcor Bett Safaris* painted on the side.'

Jamcor Bett had been one of India's most famous tiger hunters. Years earlier, there had been considerable conflict between tigers and humans. India's population had doubled in just thirty years. There was pressure on land everywhere. Forests were being cleared for farmland and building space across the country. As the forests were cut down, the tigers were displaced and many found themselves homeless.

Confrontations were inevitable, and had often led to tragedy when man came face-to-face with a wild and powerful animal like a tiger. Jamcor had been on the side of the authorities, protecting villages. Effectively, he was a bounty hunter tracking down 'troublesome' tigers. It was said that he'd killed more than forty tigers that had been classified, for one reason or another, as *man-eaters*.

Jamcor had been born in a village in the foothills of the Himalayas, and had reputed 'bush skills' that were second-to-none. The smallest broken branch or merest hint of displaced foliage would catch his eye as he moved silently through the jungle. People said he could tell the age of a paw print to within thirty minutes, just by looking at the moisture content in the exposed soil.

He also had a very keen sense of smell. He was so good that, even hours after a tiger had moved through an area, he could trace their scent and plot their exact journey; every step, through the most rugged of environments, with just a few twitches of his nostrils. He was the hunter's hunter, and with Jamcor on your trail, there was no escape.

He mainly hunted alone, but always accompanied by

his faithful Chihuahua, Bobbin (in truth, there had been several Bobbins over the years). If he were ever lost, he would send Bobbin scrambling up the nearest sal tree to work out directions. In twenty years, he had never failed to get his man (or tiger) and had frequently faced down some fearsome charges. Even now, some years after his official retirement to the seaside, he was sometimes called upon to help park authorities right across India in particularly difficult cases.

Jamcor had been at school with the Maharaja, and was an old friend. While most people called the Maharaja 'Maj' (his full title was 'Dhanesh Janesh Fitzwilliam, Maharaja of Lis'), Jamcor called him 'Bill'.

'So Bill,' he continued, 'it's definitely him, then?'

'No doubt about it,' said the Maharaja. 'Look at the photos,' and as he spoke, he pulled out the paper advertising the tigers' return to Tigeropolis, placing it squarely beside the old picture of Raj photo-bombing.

'Ah yes. No question,' said Jamcor, studying the

evidence, 'Exactly the same markings. It's Raj alright.'

They drove on. Jamcor thought for a moment, then continued, 'I think we can outfox him. He's a cheeky old fella; he couldn't resist popping out of the bushes that day and blowing a raspberry at you in that photo.

'I bet he's behind all this tourist interest now. He's obviously hooked on the celebrity of it all. That's his weakness. And that's how we'll get him.'

'What we need to do,' said Jamcor, trying to help his friend, 'is to work out where he intends to be seen… and get there first. He'll be totally unprepared: too busy worrying about his public and his profile.'

They headed straight to the Maharaja's library, and started by closely studying the maps of Tigeropolis. After about an hour, Jamcor, decisively planted his finger on a crossroads and said authoritatively, 'This is the place: Tiger's Rest. Just the spot, I would have thought.'

'I doubt it,' said the Maharaja, 'It's the name of an old teahouse that closed years ago. And anyway, I don't think they ever served tigers.'

'Hunter's Cross?' ventured Jamcor, a little half-heartedly.

'Public conveniences,' said the Maharaja gingerly, slightly worried that his old friend's tiger tracking skills had become somewhat rusty in the intervening years.

'Ah, I've got it!' said Jamcor. 'The Old Fort! You know what they say: once a soldier, always a soldier. Those military types can't keep away from military history. That's where he'll be: the fort. We've got him!'

Happy that they'd found the perfect spot, they headed outside, jumped back into Jamcor's jeep and sped off towards the Old Fort.

Uncle Raj was, indeed, on his way to the Old Fort. He'd decided it would make a great spot to be seen in the setting sun. If he timed it just right, he'd make his entrance in a shaft of sunlight while walking across the courtyard. There would be a few roars, a yawn, and then he'd end up silhouetted against the setting sun gazing out towards the river.

He'd been over to the fort earlier, and worked out exactly where he should stand at different times, marking the spots with a small chalked cross each time. He liked things to be well organized, and he liked to get there in good time too.

Across at the temple, VJ and Bittu were on their way to try to warn Raj that the Maharaja was on the hunt for him, and had even shortened the odds by bringing in Jamcor Bett to help. VJ felt sure that Raj needed to be on his guard. There wasn't a moment to lose.

Jamcor and the Maharaja arrived at the road leading to the Old Fort.

'Let's get out and walk from here,' said Jamcor. 'Bobbin, you stay here and guard the jeep, and don't let any monkeys come within fifty metres, got it?'

'Yap, yap,' barked the Chihuahua enthusiastically, as he took up his post and started patrolling back-and-forth in front of the jeep, daring anyone to come close.

'Good boy, Bobbin,' said Jamcor as the two intrepid hunters started out on their mission.

'So Bill, you think you are up to it this time?' said Jamcor, in a slightly condescending tone that the Maharaja didn't quite like.

'You'll need to crawl carefully into position. Get him in your sights. Remember the drill. Slow your breathing right down. Your heart rate and breathing need to be perfectly synchronized. At a range of more than twenty metres the slightest uncontrolled movement can mean disaster. Remember too… when the time comes, you need to pull the trigger on a slow out-breath if you're to keep everything steady.

'You may only get one chance, so make it count… but it will be worth it, I promise. Think how great it will feel to finally have that head up on your wall for all to see… Bill… you listening to me?'

'Y-yes, Jam, absolutely, sorry. I was just preparing myself,' said the Maharaja. 'I'll get that tiger if it's the last thing I do.'

'Right, let's do this thing,' said Jamcor, slapping the Maharaja hard on the back as they strode purposefully into the brush.

Expert that Jamcor was, he ensured they set off on the hunt well downwind of the ruins. Both men were careful not to make any sudden noises, carefully holding branches for each other as they moved through the bush, and avoiding treading on any twigs or dried leaves.

Suddenly, through a gap in the foliage, four-or-five hundred metres into the undergrowth, they caught a quick glimpse of a large black and orange head with a distinctive handlebar moustache. There was no question: it was Raj, about two-hundred metres distant.

They moved closer. From what they could tell, Raj was totally oblivious to their presence: in fact, he was just where Jamcor had predicted, and was far too busy rehearsing his appearance. Four steps, turn... look menacing... six steps and turn again... make some vaguely threatening grrrs... turn... now down on his rear paws, yawn, roar... make sure you show the canine teeth to good effect with a wide open mouth and a slow shake of the head... and so it went on.

The Maharaja and Jamcor continued to move stealthily. They emerged from the bush and into the high grass surrounding the fort. Inching closer, the Maharaja now had a slightly better view; but still not a clear shot, as there were a few small bushes among the grasses that obstructed his view.

'Just a little bit closer… that's it… steady now, steady,' said Jamcor to himself, as he motioned to the Maharaja to take up position next to a solitary flame tree, about one-hundred-and-thirty metres from the fort's outer wall.

The Maharaja crept into position and, half-crouched behind the tree, he got ready to take the shot. He felt his pulse racing. After all these years, he would finally get his revenge. But he needed to keep calm.

He knew the score: steady, deep breaths… just as Jamcor had said.

Try to synchronize your breathing with your heartbeat.

'Yes, steady,' he told himself, 'Wait until you see the whites of his eyes…'

Just a moment more, he thought, 'Let him turn… steady,' he knew he would only have a second, 'Now..? No wait. Wait until Raj is firmly in the cross-hairs… steady, steady… that's it, come on, perhaps now..? Yes, he's dead centre… NOW,' and ever-so-gently his index finger contracted and tightened on the trigger of the pistol grip.

'Click'

And then there was an awful moment of silence. You could hear a pin drop. Nothing seemed to move. It was as if time stood still.

'At last… I've got him!' said the Maharaja breathing again. 'The perfect shot. I've waited fifteen years for that!' he said as he put down his camera.

Jamcor smiled.

The Maharaja was ecstatic.

He turned to Jamcor and said, 'Thirty years ago that would have been a bullet straight through the head. BAM!' he said, finger extended and making an exaggerated snapping gesture, pretending to shoot Jamcor in the head.

'But you're right, Jam, thankfully the world's changed. There's no sense in shooting such a beautiful animal. A photo is just as rewarding… look,' he continued, handing Jamcor the camera, 'See, it's a perfect headshot, eyes sparkling, teeth showing. You couldn't improve on that.'

And with that, the Maharaja turned to walk back to the

jeep. 'Mission accomplished, I think. And after all those years,' he said. 'Let's get out of here. Let's go home.'

Triumphant, they climbed back into the jeep and sped off back to Lis, with broad grins, and the feeling of a job well done.

Back at his little house, the Maharaja carefully handed the camera to his faithful bearer Gautam. He told Gautam to have the photograph of Raj blown up, so that he could have it framed and hung on the wall next to all his father's old hunting trophies.

He then sat back on the sofa and turned to Jamcor.

'You know Jam... it's funny... but as I looked through the lens at that old tiger, I couldn't help thinking he must have seen a thing or two, twirly whiskers and all. And I thought to myself, what if you could talk? Yes, if only you could talk, I bet you would have a tale or two to tell...'

'Never thought about it like that before,' said Jamcor, looking at his old friend and smiling, 'I think it might be time for tea...'

THE END

Glossary

Anjali mudra – A gesture used in yoga, clasping hands together with palms together and fingers pointing up. It is a gesture of reverence.

Ashram – A spiritual retreat in India often located in rural, isolated and mountainous areas. A quiet place away from the pressures of the modern world.

Babus – Originally a term of respect, but now used as a pejorative term in reference to bureaucrats or officials. Such officials often impose (on others under their control) unnecessary rules and regulations or ways of doing things that serve no real purpose.

Bougainvillea – Colourful thorny ornamental vine that grows in hot climates.

Chhatrapati – A royal title equivalent to Emperor.

Chi/Inner chi – Life force, as described in traditional Chinese medicine.

Chowki – A small police or guard hut.

Diwali – Ancient Hindu festival – Festival of Lights – held in the autumn.

Fankle – Old fashioned Scottish word meaning entangled, or confused.

Great Mugatabala –The mythical historic text of the Maharajas of Lis.

Gulab jamun – Indian sweet or dessert.

Holi – Hindu religious festival held in the spring.

Jamun tree – Tall evergreen tree found across India. Jamun seeds are sometimes used as a medicine.

Lathi – A stout stick or baton used by Indian and Pakistan police forces. Can be up to 1.5 metres long.

Nawabs – An honorary title originally given out by Mughal Emperors, but also awarded by the British in India for services to the British colonial government.

Sitar – Indian classical, plucked string instrument, up to 21 strings. Popularised for Western audiences by the Beatles and Rolling Stones in the mid-1960s.

Sloth bear – A bear specifically found in India. Nocturnal. Shaggy black coat. Feed off ants and termites – can climb trees – sometimes go after honeycombs. Nicknamed – honey bears. Sloth bears are the only bears that carry their young on their back. Height up to about 1.8metres, weight up to 140 kgs. Live up to 40 years.

Sousaphone – A very large brass musical instrument, a type of tuba specifically designed for marching bands with the brass tubing fitting around the player. Can weigh up to 23 kgs. Mainly used in the USA.

Spicy parathas – Indian flat bread made with whole wheat flour and spices.

Talwar – Curved sword. Carried by the Maharaja's body guard.

Yoga – A spiritual, mental and physical practice that originated in India, most likely developed 500 years BC.

Yogi – A teacher who practices yoga to a high level of spiritual insight. They not only teach others the techniques of yoga but also the spirituality of yoga.

ACKNOWLEDGEMENTS

This is the second book in the *Tigeropolis* series – thanks to all who bought the first–without you we couldn't have created this new book.

Special thanks go to Kay Hutchison for backing the project and offering encouragement and advice over the many months it has taken to move from outline ideas to finished book.

There are three other key creative team members: *Tigeropolis* illustrator Matt Rowe has, once again, played a vital role in creating the world that Bittu, Matti, Tala and Uncle Raj inhabit – it's always a pleasure to see each new draft illustration come through. Ross Burridge's editorial skill, his proof reading, his help and guidance in putting together the *Tigeropolis* audiobooks and interactive video game are greatly appreciated. And thanks to Andrew Cook – our long-time collaborator, who has worked with Kay and I on a range of projects over the years – Andrew brings to the project great care and attention to detail and above all his skill in design, ensuring that the text and illustrations work together seamlessly to deliver a book I am truly proud of.

I want to mention Apinder Sidhu who offered valuable advice on the text and is helping develop our schools programme. Rebecca Souster at *Clays* (our printers) guided us carefully through the production process for which many thanks. Not forgetting *Beehive*, *Whitefox* and all at *Midas PR* for helping so enthusiastically to spread the word about *Tigeropolis*.

Finally, I would once again like to express my deep appreciation to the rangers and conservationists who protect India's wild places.

R. D. Dikstra

ABOUT THE AUTHOR

R. D. Dikstra was born and brought up in Scotland and has lived in London for most of his life. He became interested in wildlife conservation after spending two weeks whale watching in Alaska. In 1997 he helped set up a company specialising in conservation-related travel and, to this day, he continues to discover unusual places off the beaten track. He first visited a tiger park in 2009 with Julian Matthews of *Travel Operators for Tigers (TOFT)*, and immediately recognized that these were important places that needed to be protected, but also that even such serious matters could have their lighter side.

OTHER TIGEROPOLIS BOOKS

BOOK 1
BEYOND THE DEEP FOREST

BOOK 3
CAUGHT IN THE TRAP
(coming soon)

Also available on Amazon Kindle and Apple iBooks
www.amazon.co.uk/kindlebooks
www.apple.com/uk/ibooks

www.tigeropolis.co.uk

TIGEROPOLIS AUDIOBOOKS

BEYOND THE DEEP FOREST

THE GRAND OPENING
(coming soon)

CD and digital download available from
www.tigeropolis.co.uk

Read by Richard E. Grant
(Running time approx. 2hrs)

TIGEROPOLIS: THE GAME

Join Bittu and chums as they race to save the park from the bulldozers. Meet the cast of the books on an adventure through the wildest jungle!

Available on the App Store (for Apple TV and iPad).

To find out more go to…
www.tigeropolis.co.uk

TIGEROPOLIS: COMIC STRIP

Bittu and Matti love playing football, and they're currently working with the *Tigeropolis* production team to tell the story of when they had an unexpected encounter with a scout from a top football club...

Check www.tigeropolis.co.uk for more details!

Bittu

About

Born: Tigeropolis

Age (in tiger years): 1¼

Lives: in the cave complex to the north-east of the old Tigeropolis fort, together with older sister Matti and their mother Tala.

60 Second Interview: Favourites…

- Colour: Blue (and orange and black of course)
- Food: Kulfi (or any ice cream)
- Sport: Football
- Team: any team with a tiger logo (you know who you are, HCFC)
- School subject: .... (*Editor's note*: it seems Bittu was still thinking about this answer as we went to press).
- Film: *The Tigger Movie* (because the wonderful thing about tiggers…)
- TV Programme: *Dr Wu*
- Book: *Tigeropolis: Beyond the Deep Forest* (because he particularly enjoyed page 47. The most fun he's ever had!)
- Motto: 'There's another adventure around every corner.'

MATTI

About

Born: Tigeropolis

Age (in tiger years): 2

Lives: in the cave complex to the north-east of the old Tigeropolis fort, together with younger brother Bittu and their mother Tala.

60 Second Interview: Favourites...

- Colour: Pink (and orange and black of course)
- Food: Tomato bhaji
- Sport: Keeping her little brother under control. Oh and ballet!
- School subject: History
- Film: *Life of Pi* (because setting her little brother adrift in the middle of the ocean is her favourite fantasy... so much so that she's busy thinking up ways to get him to take up rowing).
- TV Programme: Any historic drama about the Mughal Empire, palaces, processions and royal events.
- Book: *Tigeropolis: Caught in the Trap* (because she's had a sneak preview of the next book, and loved hearing how Uncle Raj once again outwitted the hunters).
- Motto: 'Brain usually beats brawn... so why not listen to me in the first place, or failing that, Uncle Raj.'

See you again soon!